D1525118

The Player Hater

SARA NEY

Copyright

I think I'd miss you even if we never met.
-The Wedding Date

-

.

Prologue

JULIET

"I want you to get to know Thad better so you can know and love him the same way I do."

My best friend is watching me earnestly from across the table at our favorite restaurant; we're here so Mia can bamboozle me into getting closer to her new boyfriend, a man she's been dating for around five months now whom she wants me to bond.

Bond with how, you say? A weekend trip with them to some place she saw online and has been begging him to take her.

Why would I want to be the third wheel with just the two of them?

I stir the ice around my cocktail.

Mia thinks she can woo me with drinks at this posh bar we're sitting in—a bar that serves their concoctions in funky glasses and has the most incredible desserts—will win me over.

And under normal circumstances, she'd be right. If she were, say, asking to borrow a favorite dress or a pair of my insanely expensive high heels—I would cave at the first sip of this delicious nectar I'm drinking.

I take a sip from a glass shaped by the gods—it's shaped like a canary—filled with pink alcohol, and warms my stomach in the most scrumptious way.

But alas, Mia is not asking to borrow clothes or expensive shoes.

She's asking the impossible.

"I don't *want* to love Thad the same way you love Thad."

I'm never going to get giddy about him during a weekend getaway, no matter how hard she tries to make me and her boyfriend buddies—I'd rather love him from afar.

First of all, his name is Thad.

Secondly, he looks like a douchebag—your stereotypical professional athlete who turns into a charmer when he's around women, at least from what I can see.

Megawatt smile.

Flexes when anyone looks at his arms.

Long, flowing hair he wears in a man bun.

Textbook player.

Mia—who is still looking hopeful on the other side of the table—is blissfully swirling her gold drinking straw around a pretty glass containing a shiny liquid with edible gold glitter floating on the surface.

Eventually she sighs. "Juliet. I love you, you know I do. And I also love Thad." I cringe again at the sound of his name while she continues. "You have got to start trying—he's getting a complex and beginning to think you don't like him."

I don't like him.

At all.

And why do I care that a grown man is getting a complex because he and I are not BFF's? It's not my job to make him feel secure.

This is a him problem, not a Juliet problem.

"Why does he care if I like him or not?" Does he seriously expect all women to drop at his feet to worship him because he's good-looking, successful, and famous? Well, let me tell you something: I'm not signing up to be the Vice-President of his Fan Club anytime soon, even though my best friend is the President and currently recruiting new members.

No, thank you, sir.

"He cares because you're my best friend and he wants you to like him." This time, she delivers her sentence with an eye roll, laying on the sarcasm like syrup on waffles. "That's why we're going on this quick trip. It'll be the best way to bond instead of staying in the city with all the distractions."

I'm being difficult and we both know it.

To be honest I didn't *actually* think I was giving her boyfriend an 'I don't care for you' vibe when I was around him—I legitimately thought I was being pleasant, faking the good times and laughter for the sake of my best friend while all along finding the dude suspect.

Guess I'm not as good an actress as I thought I was.

"Mia—you know I don't want to third wheel it on a vacation with the two of you." That would be torture. "Plus, I don't have the money to go galivant to some expensive resort for the weekend." I cross my arms to punctuate my sentence, daring her to argue about my financial situation.

I will not be peer pressured into a vacation with a man I don't want to go with, although a piña colada does sound rather tasty.

"You won't be third wheeling it, and it would be his treat. All expenses paid."

Free trip?

My ears twitch.

Dammit. I would *kill* for an all-expenses paid trip.

Mia knows I'm a sucker for a bargain and obviously plans to exploit the fact.

"So now he's trying to *bribe* me?"

She laughs. "I wouldn't use the word bribe; I would use

the word coax. You're like an animal at the Humane Society that needs to be given treats so when an arm reaches into your cage, you don't gnaw it off."

I turn my nose up at the comparison. "I object at being equated to an animal in a shelter, but also—accurate." I lean forward. "Tell me more about how I won't be the third wheel. How is that possible?"

"Thad's best friend Halbrook will be there."

Halbrook? Why have I never heard that name before or met this person?

"His name is Halbrook?" I can't keep the aversion out of my voice. "What kind of name is that?" Sounds aristocratic and stuffy.

Pompous.

"Halbrook is his last name and what everyone calls him. I think his first name is Davis?"

Good god. The man's entire name is two last names.

It's too much for me to handle.

I press my lips together so the laugh doesn't burst out. "Sorry, but this is not convincing me. Why would I want to be thrown at some dude I haven't met yet, just so your boyfriend can show off for you all weekend? No thanks."

"Juliet, I'm not asking you to do it for him; I'm asking you to do it for me." Her hand crosses over to my side of the table, reaching for mine. "Please come. It's important to me."

Mia gives my hand a beseeching squeeze, her big doe eyes seemingly helpless.

I know she's not meaning to, but sonofabitch—she's good at the guilt trip, that's for sure.

Too good.

"This isn't a big ask, Juliet, it's a vacation. It'll be fun."

I hate when she's right; this isn't a big ask, plus it's a free vacation. Granted, it'll be a work in patience but a vacation nonetheless.

"Juliet and Davis? On what planet would that combination work?"

"Juliet." Her tone is so sharp I glance up from picking at the appetizer on the plate in front of me, seconds away from dropping the calamari on my tongue. "I'm not asking you to date anyone—this isn't a setup. I'm merely pointing out the fact you will not be a third wheel. Someone else will be there in the same boat and I'm not quite sure Davis likes me, either. These guys have trust issues."

I'm not sure she's being entirely honest—surely she would have mentioned these reservations about her boyfriend's best friend before?

I set the calamari onto the plate.

My shoulders slump in defeat. "Ugh, fine—I'll agree to this weekend getaway. For you—not for him—because I love *you*. But you have to promise; swear to God, hope to die, stick a needle in your eyes that you won't push me at this Halbrook Stone guy."

"Davis Halbrook."

"It sounds like a rock quarry."

Mia laughs loudly. "You need to cut it out."

I wave my hand in the air flippantly because his name does not matter. "Whatever. You have to promise this isn't a setup, and you're also not going to throw your boyfriend at me and force us to be best friends, and I don't want to date his friend, either."

I hold my hand out so she can commit to me in the only way two people can; with our pinkies wrapped around one another. We hold them a few seconds before nodding our solemn vow, the agreement more sacred than a signed contract.

"I don't need the two of you to be best friends—I am already your best friend."

"You know what I mean."

Mia beams happily, pinky promise still looped through mine. "He's a really great guy, you'll see! You'll like him. It'll be totally fun, you'll see."

She's said '*you'll see!*' twice, but who's keeping track?

I resume calamari consumption, dipping a piece first in the marinara then the ranch. "When is this fantastic extravaganza happening, anyway?"

"The weekend after my birthday."

In two weeks?

Of *course* her flashy boyfriend wants to whisk us away for her birthday, footing the entire bill to some Instagram worthy resort where they'll lie around with their perfect bodies, not gain a single ounce from sipping froofy drinks and eating whatever they want because they both work out like fiends.

I'll just be along for the ride, gaining ten pounds simply by thinking about island food and fresh waffles every morning.

Not that I'm bitter about it; I'm not, I swear.

What is wrong with you, Juliet? You should be happy for Mia, not acting like a bitter shrew.

Jealous of all the time they spend together? Pfft, me? No!

Okay, maybe I am just a teensy, weensy bit jealous if I'm being honest, but I would never in a million years say those words out loud.

No way.

I am happy for her; I just don't want her heart to get broken!

A weekend away where you can keep an eye on the guy, around the clock, will be the perfect *opportunity to do that.*

"Do you know where he wants to take you?" Us.

"Not yet—he wants it to be a surprise. He's planning the entire trip himself." She looks positively tickled pink.

Planning the trip himself?

Oh boy.

"What should I pack, any ideas?"

6

Mia mulls this over as she stirs her drink. "That's a good question—maybe a swimsuit just in case, I can't imagine we'd go anywhere that didn't have a pool? I showed him two places I thought looked amazing; one had a lake, the other has a pool."

Lake or a pool.

I concede that it does indeed sound lovely.

I muster up some enthusiasm. "Sounds like it's gonna be great!"

"So you'll really come?"

"Of course I'll come." Ugh, who could say no to that sweet, happy face? "I love you—wouldn't miss it for the world."

I down what's left in my canary shaped glass, face scrunching up like I've swallowed a lemon.

CHAPTER 1

Juliet

"When you said all expenses paid getaway, I was hoping we'd end up at a tropical destination. Or Cancun. Or, oh—I don't know. *Fiji*."

My best friend laughs at me as I step down from the black SUV and survey the same surroundings I've been watching through the tinted window on our shuttle ride from the airport; acre after acre of wooded trees coupled with the overwhelming scent of pine.

Washington nature at its finest.

A lake shimmers in the background through even more trees.

And more trees.

"Are you sure we didn't take a wrong turn somewhere? Perhaps while the plane was zipping us past California?"

We'd passed the cutest little town on our drive here about twenty-five minutes back. There wasn't much to it but a restaurant, a bank, a bar, and a gas station—but quaint, just the same. Anyway, it was hard to see where we are in the fading sunlight.

"Where on earth are we?"

Mia glances down at the screen of her phone then holds it up into the air, squinting at it. "I have horrible reception here but the guys are already here somewhere. At least Thad is."

"That's what I'm trying to figure out—where here is."

"Did you not see the big wooden sign at the entrance?" She holds her phone into the air as if a better signal were going to beam down to her.

Um no—unless it was a sign for Disneyland, I completely missed it. Disney, by the way, happens to be one of Mia's favorite escapes we go to *at least* once a year, spending a day at Disneyland California Adventure and a day at the hotel pool. Usually it's the last place on earth I want to be but I'd swap this woodsy murder trap for a park full of people in a heartbeat.

"I am so glad he decided on this place. At first I was thinking he'd choose Hawaii, but I'd seen a sponsored ad for this place too and fell in love." She spins, hiking boots crunching into the gravel as she attempts a pirouette.

Hiking boots?

No one told me to pack hiking boots!

Shit.

"Why did I think we were coming to the tropics? Why! I had such high hopes I packed three swimsuits just in case. It's not too late to turn around and head to the Caribbean you know." I hike the laptop bag further up on my shoulder and scowl at her through the dark lenses of my sunnies.

"You're so funny." My best friend giggles. "You'll still have a chance to put one of those suits on if the lake isn't freezing cold."

Great. "I'm not sure the lake is happening for me. Haven't you ever heard of shrinkage?"

"Only guys have shrinkage."

"And me—I have big dick energy, remember?"

Behind us, someone clears their throat. "Ladies, there's a

driver on his way to come grab you and take you to the cabins. They should be here any second." Our driver then busies himself by opening the back of the shuttle and hauling our suitcases out the back, one heave at a time.

Mia has one.

One suitcase and a tote.

I have two suitcases and it appears that while I was packing, I was prepping for a month-long excursion, filling it with day dresses, skirts for fancy dinners, cover-ups, cute matching pajamas—and every lotion and potion that goes into my rigorous skincare routine.

Hey. Wrinkles don't disappear themselves, they have to be babied, and I wanted to pack anything and everything I might need for a fun, adventure filled weekend.

This is an adventure alright.

The engine of a vehicle echoes in the still dusk air, the sun making a slow descent in the sky as an ATV materializes from a trail in the near distance.

It's a four-seater, I notice as it gets closer. "It's like an Uber in the north woods," I joke.

Our shuttle driver begins stacking our bags into the back of the vehicle as the guy climbs out and comes around to introduce himself.

"Missus Watley? Mia?" His hand isn't sure which one to shake until Mia grabs hold and gives it a firm squeeze. "Welcome. I'm Ben Sutter, the innkeeper and well, the concierge as well. Thad is already waiting for you back at the cabins, making sure everything is perfect. If you both want to hop on into the Gator, we'll be at the site in a few short minutes."

"The site?"

After thanking our shuttle driver and tipping him, we climb in, waving one last time before my eyes fully digest our surroundings.

"...obviously I'll be here to take you into town if you need anything, and of course, I can easily make you reservations for any of the restaurants in town." I can barely make out Ben's words as we crunch along the trail, motor and gravel and wind drowning out his welcome speech. "...also board games and cards. Then again, you folks might enjoy the quiet time."

Mia is nodding her head along enthusiastically.

I've always known she has wanted to take a trip and "rough it" for a weekend—she has a very stressful advertising job; works crazy long hours and manages several high-profile accounts. My best friend rarely has time off that when she does, Mia tends to spend it shopping, going to the spa, or getting her hair and eyelashes done.

So this solitude we're about to embark on? I'm sure it's a welcome change.

It's wonderful seeing her so happy but at the same time, I see nothing but blue skies and trees; not a piña colada or hammock in sight.

I'm not spoiled, *honestly.*

I just wasn't expecting this type of trip and have the fancy dresses to prove it; I totally had it in my brain that we were going somewhere hot.

Reframe, Juliet.

Reframe.

This is a good thing—Mia needs to relax and unwind. And sure, she could have done that in a pool with a swim up bar, but that's neither here nor there. Or a resort with a spa, perhaps?

Pfft.

Those come and go; the threat of poison ivy you never forget.

We approach what Ben referred to as "the site," six shiny and modern airstream campers converted into cabins and arranged in a half circle facing a massive lake. Each one has its own private deck and striped awning, along with a sliding glass door facing the lake and a flickering lantern next to its entrance.

The camper—or, let's be real: glamper—in the center has a beautiful wildflower arch around its small door at the front, dozens of candles glowing. On the picnic table, on the steps, in the sand going down to the water.

"Flameless," Ben says under his breath in case we get any ideas about burning actual candles at the campsite.

Mia gasps as her boyfriend comes out the door holding a bouquet in one hand, crowning my bestie with a small, hand-woven wreath in her hair, planting a kiss on her mouth.

"Happy birthday, baby."

She flies into his arms.

"It was my birthday last week, you goof," my friend sobs happily, melting into his embrace. "You are too good to me."

So tiny compared to his massive frame, Mia all but vanishes into Thad's body, his arms like two giant sausages, stuffed into a long-sleeve cotton tee, aka: meat casings. The dude is way too big to be wearing tight clothes but I suppose it's not easy finding things that fit.

I'll give him a pass even though he's yet to acknowledge my presence.

I shift on my heels as they stand there, continuing to hug, Thad cooing in my best friend's hair—she'd thrown it into a cute ponytail on the shuttle ride to the resort, always looking tidy. Jet-black hair, petite, and sweet as apple pie, I understand his attraction to her but cannot seem to trust the guy.

Something about him throws me off and I'm glad to have the chance to observe him over the weekend.

He kisses the top of her head, then practically pets it, hand running through her silken hair.

Break it up you two, some of us are embarrassed to be standing here while you paw at one another, it's on the tip of my tongue to say. I'm hungry and tired, and would love to climb into a shower and into the one pair of warm pajamas I'm glad I brought.

Hallelujah!

The whole scene is vomit inducing, heart pounding romance and although I hadn't wanted to be here, I *am* glad I get to see Mia so happy.

I just hope it ends the way she wants it to.

Thad is talking into her hair. "I'm so glad you made it. I'm so sorry I wasn't at the airport to come get you but I had so many things to get done here and things to grab in town so you'd be comfortable."

More sobbing from Mia.

More kissing.

Ben waits behind me for the right moment to mutter out an awkward, "Okay, well—I'll just put their bags inside their cabins for you Thad."

I clear my throat.

Clear it again to get the lovey-dovey couple's attention. "Uh, hello? Some of us would like to freshen up?"

"Oh shit, you're right. Of course you ladies want to freshen up. Sorry, I'm off in my own little world." He winks at me as if we're co-conspirators. "Halbrook isn't here yet, so we'll just do our thing."

I refrain from groaning out loud as he steps forward to hug me, too, though my hug isn't nearly as warm as the one he gave his girlfriend. Obviously.

Hmm. "Which camper is yours?"

"Oh, we're not staying in one of these. Our place is over there."

I follow his extended arm; he's pointing into the woods, to a tent rising from the earth in a different area completely. But not just any old tent. No, this one is one of those posh setups with a chandelier, an actual bed, and a sitting area.

The kind you see on television on one of those swanky travel shows.

Ugh. Jealous!

"You're sleeping in there?" I glance over at the campers. "Where am I sleeping?"

"You're in the Happy Camper—the one with the flowers around the door." Thad beams. "Babes and I still need a kitchenette to use and stuff, and we can all use the porch at night for sitting around and looking at the water. It'll be so peaceful." He has his hulky arm around Mia's waist and he gives it a squeeze.

All I hear is 'Babes and I.'

I shake the words out of my skull and smile, hefting the carry-on bag on my shoulder; I feel so ridiculous having brought all this crap now.

"Oh, sure. The Happy Camper sounds delightful."

I can do this—I can totally do this. It's not as if we're roughing it in an actual tent; I can survive living in the cute glamper a few short nights while my friend stays in the canvas tent outfitted for a Kardashian.

I gaze at it longingly, with its own flameless trail of candles flickering in the night, bend vine chairs, steamer trunk coffee table and hanging lanterns.

Sigh.

It is crazy romantic, the entire thing glowing softly in the dark.

My own little camper is cute, too, and I approach it with Ben, as my best friend and her boyfriend head toward their digs.

"Here you are. Cozy as a bedbug," Ben jokes before seeing my face. "Kidding. Just kidding, there are no bedbugs. We routinely check between each and every guest."

I nod with a heavy swallow and a nervous laugh. "I'm not worried."

Bedbugs are probably the least of my problems; surely there are creatures and critters larger than that lurking in every crack and crevasse. Besides, I once spent the night in a motel infested with roaches—I think I can handle a few creepy crawlies.

Maybe.

Ben carries my giant suitcases along the path to the door of the shiny, silver camper, vintage in its aesthetic but modern in every other way. Running water, electricity. A flat television mounted above the cabinets in the small "living room" slash kitchen.

Ben doesn't follow me inside—it's cramped, and he's a stranger—but he does stand at the entrance, waiting to see if there's anything additional I require before retracing his steps and firing up the off-roading vehicle he dropped us off with.

I listen as the engine noise fades into the distance, my eyes catching glimpses of the glowing tent out the window to the back of my glamper.

The noise is deafeningly silent.

Nary a peep, not even from a cricket—

Never mind, there goes one.

Hefting one of my suitcases atop the small kitchen table, I carefully unzip it so it doesn't implode, the mess inside making me cringe. Security must have gone through it, for clothes are unfolded and tossed back inside haphazardly—not the way I'd painstakingly rolled and packed them the day before so they would fit like a puzzle.

I remove my toiletries, grateful the bag has a hook perfect for the back of the bathroom door, with its utter lack of counter space. Put the travel size bottles of shampoo and conditioner in the minuscule shower.

Slippers go on my feet. Robe goes in the bedroom.

Silk pillowcase goes on the pillow *and I swear I'm not high-maintenance*, I just like to be comfortable! I thought I was going to a spa in the Caribbean for a long weekend, okay? Sheesh.

I thought perhaps everyone would gather at the bonfire that is simmering on the sandy beach near the lake, but when I get a text from Mia saying *'Get a good night's rest, we have a busy day tomorrow!'*, I know we won't be outside tonight singing kumbaya into the wee hours of the morning.

The television works, but doesn't have Netflix. Instead of trying to harness technology while in the middle of the woods, I take out the few magazines and crossword puzzles stored in my carry-on, and make myself comfortable on the bed.

———

"...*Is she dead?*"

"...*No way—she's definitely alive. Her chest is moving up and down.*"

"...*Maybe we should check just to be sure. We can hold a mirror under her nose. If it fogs up, we'll know.*"

"...Mia, I could hear her snoring before we even walked inside."

Snoring?

What? Who's snoring?

I wipe at the corner of my mouth and feel moisture. Ew, is that drool?

"Oh yeah, she's definitely alive."

I feel a finger poking into my ribcage. "Up and at 'em, Sleeping Beauty, your new roommate has arrived!"

Roommate? What is this nonsense?

"Eh?" Startled by the unfamiliar male voice, I blink open my eyes, staring blankly at the unfamiliar ceiling. Where the hell am I? Why is it so bright in here?

"Juliet, wake up. You've slept half the day away."

Oh shit, that's right; I'm camping in the middle of God's

SARA NEY

Green Earth, with naught but a bag full of beach cover-ups and flirty athleisurewear.

I roll to the side, grumping at the sound of my best friend's voice. "Slept the day away? Ha. I never sleep past seven."

Even half passed out I'm argumentative.

Mia huffs as she jostles me again. "Well it's past ten. We've already had breakfast."

Already had breakfast!

I frantically shoot up as if someone has taken a fire and lit it under my ass.

"Ten? Why didn't anyone wake me up!" How could she eat without me! She knows I need food first thing in the morning, as soon as I peel my eyes open!

She *knows* this! I'm a complete monster until I've had sustenance! I literally need a three-course breakfast before I can start my day.

"I tried calling and texting. I was actually starting to get worried that you were dead." Mia chews on a fingernail behind the man who's impolitely hovering over my bed as if I'm a spectacle.

Although, to his credit, he *does* look concerned.

Bah! He needs to go away!

Pulling the blankets up farther so they're covering my chest, I narrow my eyes at him. "Stop looking at me."

Shit, was that rude? What if he works for the glampground and I just insulted him? I hate having bad manners, but it's not like *staring* is polite.

I backpedal. *Sort of.* "What I meant to say was—can I help you with something?" I pause. "Sir."

He grins at me.

I scowl at his audacity. "I can't get out of bed with y'all crowding me—give a girl some room, would you?"

"Did she just say y'all? I thought you were both originally

18

from Illinois," the behemoth interloper drawls, most definitely from the south or thereabouts.

It's too early for me to be sleuthing his origins.

I close my eyes again as they continue talking about me behind my back. Or, right in front of my closed eyelids.

"She is from Illinois—I don't know why she insists on saying y'a—"

"Um, hello!" I put my arm up and wave a hand in the air. "I'm literally lying right here. Could you all get out of my room, so I can get dressed?"

I hear a male voice chuckling.

Mia gives a small, apologetic gasp. Flutters her hands. "Juliet is right; everyone give her space. We shouldn't have come inside anyway."

"I had to bring in my stuff." The strange dude turns, presenting me with a view of his ass. "And who said she could hog the entire bed?"

Hog the entire bed? There is only one bed and it's mine.

Nevertheless, my gaze travels upward, foggy as it may be. Up the tight back end to broad shoulders and a thick neck, the telltale sign of a fresh, new, haircut at its base.

He glances at me over his shoulder, eyebrows raising when he catches me staring.

"Come on, Halbrook—I want to run and reserve a boat for later, I hear they stock this lake with bass."

Davis.

Boat.

Bass.

Oh my god—that guy is Davis Halbrook?

That...that...lumbersexual with the plaid shirt, tight ass and lingering stare?

I crane my neck, waiting to climb out of the bed until I hear the screen door slam for the last time, eyes homing in on the duffle bag in the kitchenette.

Scurrying up, I scramble to close the actual door, locking myself inside so I can rinse off and change, brush my teeth and the whole bit, before making a late-morning appearance outside.

I can't believe I slept this late—I never sleep this late!

Must be the fresh air.

And the travel. And the anxiety.

Rooting through my bags, I unearth the only casual things I brought—jeans and a lightweight crewneck sweatshirt—and throw that on with sneakers.

I wish I'd known we were coming to this place; I would have packed more appropriate attire. These sundresses certainly aren't going to cut it; I'll look like a complete asshole gathered 'round the bonfire wearing pastel pink florals.

I can't live in these same jeans and sweatshirt for the next three days, but I may have to.

One night down, three to go...

Hair in a ponytail, I finally emerge from my hovel, not the least bit bright eyed and bushy tailed, searching for my friend. Raising my nose in the air on my way down the little path to her tent, the lingering smell of bacon hits my senses, along with the aroma of coffee.

My stomach grumbles.

"Juliet!" Mia spies me before I see her, appearing from inside her cute, canvas tent, side-stepping the steamer trunk coffee table on its wooden deck so she can envelope me in a hug. "There you are!"

I kiss her cheek when I hug her back.

"Did you get a good night's rest? I was so worried when you weren't up bright and early."

"Yes, I think I slept good? I must have been out like a light."

"It's the fresh air for sure."

I nod, taking a sip from the coffee she hands me. "Thank you, ugh, I need this."

"Don't thank me, thank Ben. That man is an angel."

I raise a tired brow and continue sipping as we walk into her tent.

"Maybe he's single?" Mia muses out loud.

"Please stop trying to set me up with any man that has a pulse. I'm not moving to the wilds of wherever this place is to be some dude's sidekick in the great outdoors." More sipping. "I'm what you would call indoorsy."

"I just want you to know I got your back," she laughs, plopping down in a chair, gesturing toward the food laid out on the coffee table. "Here, let's sit down and eat. I made you a plate when you didn't show up for breakfast—the vultures were circling and I knew there wouldn't be anything left."

"Vultures?! What vultures?" My head spins around anxiously, waiting for the predatory birds to come flocking down from the trees over our heads.

Mia rolls her eyes. "I'm talking about the other guests. They had a small spread between seven and nine, and everyone swooped in—lucky you, you missed the mob."

"Other guests?"

"Yes. You missed that rush too, a small caravan arrived early this morning. Everything was set out as a warm welcome —it was really nice, but would be great if we were the only ones here, you know? Quiet and private." She steals a piece of bacon and chomps on it. "That's why Thad and Davis ran to sign us up for two boats—there isn't going to be anything left."

Two boats? Um. *What's that supposed to mean?*

I assume Thad is renting some boat so we can do a sunset wine cruise, or sunbathe tomorrow—only one of which I'm well prepared for considering the swimsuits I have jammed into my suitcases.

I eat my bacon and listen to her chatter.

"...And you've already met Halbrook, so that's out of the way."

I refuse to call him by his last name. "Met Davis? When?"

"This morning when we came and woke you up?"

"That was Davis?" Oh Jesus. "I wasn't still asleep and dreaming that all happened? You know I can't fully focus until I've had my coffee. I'm like the Crypt Keeper in the morning, Mia!"

"You weren't that out of it, stop being so dramatic. Who did you think that was hovering over you, another grounds keeper?"

I look like total shit, and I only know this because I just caught a glance of myself in the mirror they have above that cute little bureau in Mia and Thad's glamping tent. Below it is one of those old-fashioned wash basins.

"Ew, I look hideous. I cannot believe he saw me like this."

Not that I care. I don't know him.

"You don't look hideous, stop being so dramatic."

This from the woman who was probably up before dawn to wash and air dry her hair, and apply makeup so skillfully it doesn't look like she's wearing any at all.

"You clearly don't love me at all," I sniffle.

"He doesn't care what you look like."

"Gee, thanks."

She laughs. "What I meant was, the two of you aren't here to be set up. You're here because Thad wants the two of you to be friends, so we can all do more things together like one big happy family."

"Okay fine—but couldn't we have just like, gone to dinner or something? Was it necessary to be this extreme?"

My best friend shrugs. "I can't pretend to know what goes on in his pretty little head half the time, but this is what he planned. I wouldn't have chosen this location for a first meet up—knowing how you are—but now we have to make the best of it." She glances behind her into the cute tent and gestures. "I mean, how adorable is this? And it's only for a few more nights and then we can go to the spa and get facials and massages and everything will be right with the world again." She nabs the coffee I just sat down and steals a drink. "Do you think I love the idea of being stuck in a cabin without the use of my flat iron? No."

"But you're the one who wanted to come here!"

"Right, but I wasn't at all prepared! You can't just spring this on someone." She leans forward and touches my leg. "Don't tell him I said that, his feelings would be so hurt."

I nod.

Her secret is safe with me.

"I'm going to be re-wearing this same pair of leggings and tee shirt this entire weekend, most of what I brought was for a romantic weekend somewhere warm. Not that it's cold here, but you know—there's less sand than I was anticipating."

"Oh my god—same."

"What on earth made me think we were coming somewhere warm? Seriously, I got so caught up in the idea that I lost my common sense."

"Of the two of us, you're definitely the one who's more overzealous." Mia giggles softly.

"When you didn't say exactly where we were coming and only gave me tiny hints about it, I filled in the gaps myself." I pause, remembering our previous conversations. "When you said there were twinkling lights in the trees—I assumed you meant palm trees. When you said we were going to sit under the stars and gaze—I assumed you meant stars over the ocean."

"That sounds like you, always letting that imagination run away with you." Mia pauses and glances over. "Um. Didn't you realize you weren't headed south when you arrived at the airport and boarded a plane headed west?"

I thought that was weird?

"I'm an English teacher, not a Geography teacher."

I'm also horrible at math, science, and astronomy.

We share a laugh. "So now what?"

Mia sits back and crosses her legs. "Now we wait for the guys to get back from their errands; hopefully we're able to score a boat. I think there is a bonfire tonight with the other campers."

I glance over to my silver airstream and notice people milling about now that it's later in the morning—people that were not there last night when we arrived.

Awesome—more people! Other signs of life mean we're not stuck here alone, just the four of us.

If Davis is anything like his buddy Thad—a pampered former playboy who loves attention and the spotlight—it's going to be a practice in patience.

Thank god I only have to see him when we're doing activities...

CHAPTER 2
Davis

"Uh—what are you doing in here? You can't just barge in."

Juliet is back in her camper—correction: *our* camper—hands on her hips, standing in the doorway glaring daggers in my direction. For a dainty little thing, Mia's best friend sure seems angry.

Maybe she doesn't like being woken from a dead sleep while she's drooling and snoring?

In any case, it appears she has a chip on her shoulder, or maybe she hates men?

Who knows.

I was in the process of unpacking my things from the duffle bag I brought when she burst through the door, back from reserving the boat and a few other things for the four of us to do over the long weekend.

"I didn't just barge in. I was invited." I pause, folding a hoodie before tucking it inside a drawer. "And hello to you, too—nice to meet you, I'm Davis."

I walk over and hold my hand out but the stubborn woman just stares down at it rudely.

"Invited by who? And how did you get in, I locked the door when I left."

I reach into the pocket of my jeans and dangle the key in front of my face. "Oh look, I have one, too."

"Why?"

She hasn't left the doorway, her entire frame taking up the entire minute area with a defensive stance.

"Because this is where I'm living for the next couple days?"

"Living here?" Her mouth parts and I can see the shock on her expression. "Like—*here* here? In here. This camper?"

I chuckle. "I wouldn't be putting my underwear in the drawers if I wasn't staying in here."

Her eyes flicker to the kitchen drawer I just recently closed, it's still open an inch or two, revealing my red boxer briefs.

Juliet shakes her head, ponytail swinging. "No one told me I would be sharing a room with some random guy."

"Good news, I'm a decent human, so you can rest easy."

She laughs. "You're not sleeping in here."

She's so bossy. So direct.

"Why not?"

"'Cause—this is *my* place."

Her place?

I cluck my tongue and grin at her. "Now you sound spoiled and I'm sure that's not the case," I lie, deciding she's most certainly acting like a spoiled brat. What's the big deal if we sleep in the same camper, it's not as if we're going to fool around and get romantic?

If Juliet is always this high-strung, then she's definitely not my type. I like good-natured, easygoing, and fun-loving women—not uptight hall monitors.

"I'm sorry, but that's not for you to decide."

"Uh—yeah it is. I'm a female, you're a male, I don't know you—you're not sleeping here. End of story."

"Not to be a dick, but that's not really for you to decide. If you don't want to share a room with someone, perhaps you should go see if you can find another place to stay."

Her jaw literally drops open and a squeak of air puffs out.

"Besides, why should I be the one to leave? This is a two-person camper and I was under the impression, and *fine* with it, I would be sharing—you didn't actually expect Thad was going to fork over a few thousand dollars, so you could be in your own room, did you?"

I can see from her expression the answer is yes—yes, she did think she'd be in her own camping space.

"You should chat with Mia, I guess, and figure it out." I go about ignoring her, but it's hard—she's kind of adorable when she's prissy and pretty, and I'm guessing under that prickly exterior lies a heart of gold.

But maybe I'm just naïve. I tend to think the best of everyone and where does it get me?

Nowhere.

I'm still single, with zero kids and no dog.

I know what you're thinking: poor guy doesn't even have a dog?! How can that be?

Alas, it's true—I'd love one, obviously, but would love a partner to shoulder the responsibility with and also take it to the dog park with me, because dogs need friends, too.

"You look awfully miffed. Are you sure we can't be interim best friends because our best friends are dating?"

"I don't know what you're talking about. Interim best friends?"

"Sure," I say. "Friends for the weekend. We'll pretend for the sake of Mia and Thad that we like each other and no one will be the wiser."

"I'm not good at pretending," she deadpans, looking hella tired despite the coffee mug in her hand.

She taps on the ceramic with well-manicured, light pink nails.

"Not good at pretending?" I bet you a million dollars she's pretended to have plenty of orgasms.

I bite my tongue, folding a pair of joggers I've decided to leave in my duffle, kicking the entire bag beneath the rickety kitchen table—if I sat on it, the entire thing would collapse beneath my weight, not that I've thought about sitting on it to see if I actually weigh too much to collapse it.

I'd done a bit of snooping around while Juliet was having breakfast with Mia, checking out all the cubbies and nooks and crannies and concluding that this place is cute as a button; I'm definitely not moving out of this little slice of heaven in the boonies.

Besides, in a few hours after spending a bit of time with me, she'll be singing a different tune, not spearing me with her murder face.

She'll be half in love with me like they all are.

If only they loved me for me.

Ha!

"No. I'm not good at pretending and I'm not going to fake liking you for the sake of some guy I hardly know."

The socks in my hand are wadded up as I hold them above my duffle, suspended in mid-air. "Are you talking about me, or Thad?"

"Thad." Juliet hesitates. "And you, of course. I'm not here to be anyone's best friend except Mia's—she deserves a decent, honest guy and I'm here to make sure that's what Thad is."

"You don't think Thad actually cares for Mia?" This is news to me. "Why would you think otherwise? Has he given you a reason not to trust him?"

I've never known my friend to be a cheater or a player—Thaddeus Dumont is a one-woman guy as far as I'm concerned. I've never seen him sleep around or step out behind anyone's back; not that he's had many relationships. For the longest time, his career was number one—only recently has he been giving actual thought to his future and life after football.

Thad wants a family, kids, a picket fence and two and a half dogs.

Wait.

Two and a half kids?

Whatever, he wants both in however many quantities.

Juliet is shaking her head. "No, he hasn't. But have you seen him?"

Er. Yes? "I have to stare at his ugly mug more often than I'd like. What does that have to do with anything?"

"The man is a god—women must chase him and throw themselves at his feet. Do you know how much willpower that takes?" She snorts. "What man can resist a groupie."

Now I'm the one snorting. "Um, plenty of them. Fuc—er, banging your way around town gets old after a while. He's not a rookie anymore; he's been playing ball for years and that's his job. He doesn't play the sport for the women." I toss the socks back into my bag and rest my hands on my hips, facing her. "Isn't it a little too early in the day to be so cynical, what is the actual problem? Are you pissed we're not at the spa?"

She kind of has "spa" written all over her, not 'I'm a roughing it in the woods' kind of gal. Her non-response is all the answer I need.

"Let me get this straight—you're here to basically spy on Mia and Thad and try to trap him into cheating on her?"

"No! I'm not trying to trap him into cheating with me— are you implying that I would hit on him? Ew, gross."

So is she implying that she wants him to hit on her?

"Weird, because that's exactly how it sounds. Am I gonna have to keep an eye on you while you're keeping an eye on him?"

I try to laugh the idea off, but there's an element of truth to it and we both know it. Juliet didn't look shady when I was standing over her this morning, but now that I'm looking at her in the doorway of the camper, she looks angrier. Frustrated for no reason. Sulky.

She has a mug full of coffee in her belly—isn't caffeine supposed to make people happier?

Or at least more alert and wide awake?

"You don't have to keep an eye on me. All I said was he is too good-looking and handsome..."

"Too good-looking and handsome for what? Fidelity? Loyalty? Do you look at me and think the same thing?" I shoot her a megawatt grin aimed to charm and resume unpacking my things. Her eyes trail to the duffle bag resting on the kitchen table and she scowls again.

"Hey, easy on the unpacking. We haven't resolved the living situation yet."

I laugh. "Let me make one thing clear; I'm a super chill dude. Easygoing. Calm and collected. I'm thinkin' maybe you should try acting the same way—you know—like an adult and not an immature high school student who gets squeamish at the idea of being in the same room with a guy." I refuse to look at her. "I'm not going to try anything, I'm going to keep my hands to myself. Are you the type of girl who giggles when a guy says something flirtatious? Because if that's the case you really should grow up."

Her mouth falls open wider than it was before.

I smirk. "Yeah, that's what I thought."

"Are you implying the reason I don't want to share a camper with you is because I am immature?"

I nod. "That's exactly what I'm implying. You're a big girl, put on your big girl panties and deal with the situation. If you go out there and complain to your best friend that you have to share a room with me, you're gonna come off as being really ungrateful. More ungrateful than you actually sound, and I have a feeling you wouldn't want Mia to think that, would you?"

Juliet narrows her eyes in my direction, steam practically rising out of her nose. "They told me over and over what a nice guy you are."

"So now I'm not a nice guy because I refuse to kowtow to you? That because you're *telling* me to leave, I should leave? Now you one hundred percent sound spoiled." I pause. "Where do you suppose I should sleep? On the ground outside, in front of the door? Or maybe a hammock in a tree? Or wait—how about I go on down to Cabin Four and see if they'll harbor me? Newsflash: the place is booked solid."

Juliet's nostrils flare. "You've called me spoiled twice and I'm offended by that. You shouldn't make me feel like shit because I'm hesitant to share a room with a complete stranger."

"Out of everything I just said, that's your takeaway?" I have no intention of standing here bickering. It's a gorgeous day and the sun is out. Plus, Thad and I managed to score a boat for tomorrow and we have that to look forward to.

I click my tongue. "Sounds to me like you don't trust your friend's judgment. She has met me dozens of times and trusts me with you."

For the briefest of seconds Juliet hangs her head and shoulders in shame and I can see the regret washing over her. The moment lasts in the blink of an eye, over and done with, in a flash, and before I know it, she's huffing out loud.

Squaring her shoulders, she looks me dead in the eye.

"Fine. We'll share this camper—but keep your mitts off of me. Don't get any ideas."

I'd love to throw a barb back at her in the form of chuckling, but fight the power—the truth is, I think Juliet is pretty darn adorable. I happen to love the fact that she's outspoken and telling me what's on her mind and is far from shy.

It's an attractive quality that I respect and wish more women were like her.

"We haven't even started the day; let's not get off on the wrong foot. Want to start over?" I hold my hand out as an offering, expecting her to take it and shake it.

She stares down. "What's that?"

"It's my hand?" She has me doubting myself.

"What's it doing?"

"Waiting for you."

Juliet slaps it, in a pancake low five, scooting around me. "Happy now?"

"Not really—I was looking for a handshake, so we can seal the deal."

"What deal?"

"Fresh start."

She hums, setting her coffee mug on the counter in the kitchenette, letting herself into the bathroom and closing the door behind her. Two seconds later, she sticks her head back out.

"There's no fan in here." It's an announcement filled with dismay.

"So?"

Juliet watches me pointedly—so pointedly, I get uncomfortable. "Sooo...."

"*Sooo*..." I repeat in the exact same tone and inflection.

This is a fun game.

Juliet blinks; clears her throat.

"Am I supposed to know what's going on right now?" Because I don't. I'm a guy and she's giving me way too much credit. The last time I read minds was never.

"I need to use the bathroom."

"So?"

"If you say *so* one more time, I swear to God..."

"So what if you have to go to the bathroom? Go." Pause.

"Wait—are you worried I'm going to bust in on you? That bathroom is dinky, I know two of us are never going to fit. You are totally safe, I will not be busting in." I glance up from my task and look at her face. "Are you blushing?"

She blushes harder.

What's her deal? Why is she being weir—

Ohhh.

I get it now, she has to take a shit and doesn't want me to hear or smell it. Ha!

The good news is, those toilets aren't filled with water, and they're not porcelain. The chances of me hearing her do the deed are slim, but that doesn't seem to matter.

Take a hint, Davis.

She wants me gone—out of the cabin, out of hearing distance.

"Okay. Right. I need to take a piss so maybe I'll go...find, a...um, tree or something somewhere. Plenty of them, eh?"

Stop talking, Davis.

I make a show of closing the drawer I'm digging in and zipping up my duffle, tossing it to the kitchen bench and dusting off my palms on the leg of my jeans.

Make for the trail outside and meander down it, greeting the few people I meet along the way.

"Hey there, good morning," I tell a good-looking older couple as I get closer to the shoreline where the piers are. Thinking I might park my ass in one of the Adirondack chairs arranged at the end of one of the piers to kill time while I wait for Thad, Mia, and Juliet to finish whatever they're doing so we can hang out as a group. Well, I know what Juliet is doing, but don't want to think about what Thad and Mia are up to.

"Hi!" The woman sizes me up and down. "Headed to the water? We were just down there—it's breathtaking."

"Yes, ma'am," I nod, eyes already taking in the scenery and loving it.

The woman has her partner—husband, boyfriend?—by the arm and squeezes his bicep. "Did you hear that Erik, he called me ma'am."

I was raised in the south; I like to think I have passable manners and great etiquette. I say please, thank you, and hold doors when people are entering a building at the same time I am. I carry groceries and say 'bless you' if someone sneezes. So yeah—I'm going to call this woman ma'am.

It's respectful.

Her eyes are lit up like Christmas trees. "We heard Thad Dumont was here, but they didn't mention that two football players were here this weekend. Do you play football too? You're *so* big!"

She drags her gaze up and down my torso again, eyes pausing in the center of my legs. Brazen, considering her partner is standing beside her, probably wondering what else on me is big, too.

"I'm retired." I reach forward and extend my hand to the guy. "Davis Halbrook."

"Retired!" she exclaims. "You can't be in your thirties!"

"Thirty-three," I amend. And yeah, that sounds young to retire, but not when it comes to football. My body is already beat to shit and I pay for it every day.

"I've heard of you," the man says, his legs bare despite the chill in the air. "How are you enjoying retirement?"

"I'm in finance now, so there's still no sitting around." Finance sounds boring to most people—compared to playing professional football—but I have a Business Degree after playing college ball that comes in handy now that I'm off the playing field. Never thought I would need Plan B (an actual degree), but here we are, the ripe old age of thirty-three, with a bad knee, bad back, and more concussions than I can keep track of.

Many of my clients—I manage retirement accounts and investments—are athletes and retired athletes.

"You're here with Dumont and his girlfriend?" the couple asks.

"Yup, she's always wanted to come to a place like this and found this campground on social media."

The woman—who still hasn't introduced herself—titters. "This isn't my idea of a romantic weekend, but we had to compromise. Erik wanted to spend the weekend at a dude ranch in Wyoming but had to settle for a campground with Wi-Fi and electricity. He can ride horses tomorrow. Best of both worlds."

"Roughing it in style." I nod with a grin. "I'm sorry, I didn't catch your name," I say to the woman. "You're Erik and you are...?"

"Celeste. But everyone calls me Cookie."

Cookie.

I refuse to ask the origin for the nickname and how it came about. Definitely sounds snooty, though, she doesn't look it?

"Are you here with anyone special?" Cookie coos.

"No—there are four of us in our party, but Juliet and I just met."

Cookie's eyes light up. "Oh—Juliet. What a *romantic* name! We can't wait to meet her, can we, Erik?" Another squeeze to her partner's arm, the pair of them positively radiating sex.

I know swingers when I see them and make a mental note to be less friendly next time we bump into one another.

"I'm not sure Juliet is going to live up to her name," I blurt out, still butt hurt that she tried kicking me out of the camper before even meeting me.

I'm a great dude!

Wouldn't hurt a fly, let alone some woman I've only just

met. She's the girlfriend of my best friend's girlfriend; it was my intention to take great care of her and be her friend when *her* friend was busy getting romantic with mine.

Oh well, some friendships aren't meant to be.

They're called friendshits, and I have a feeling the one with Juliet and I is going to stink.

Juliet's loss, not mine.

I plan to make the most of this glorious weekend—the great outdoors, surrounded by friendly faces and my best buddy. That's winning at life right there.

I continue my way down to the lakefront, a little bit bummed that there are no other people down here—despite the swinger-vibe I got, Cookie and Erik seemed really nice and I'm looking forward to meeting the other folks staying with us in the other cabins. On the water, a few ducks call, their squawks echoing. In the distance, I spy several homes sprinkled in the woods.

I've always wanted to have a lake house, but never saw the point in having one as a single man. I get enough alone time, why would I subject myself to complete silence in the middle of the woods? I much prefer the sound of a slamming screen door and the laughter of kids. Maybe a dog barking. Splashing.

Yeah, I totally want a wife and kids. I've been looking for love, just haven't found anyone—at least, not the right one. Lots of gold diggers, cleat chasers, and fame whores—but not one woman with a heart of gold, I could bring home to my mom or the places I volunteer.

Bending, I pick a pebble off the shore and lob it sideways onto the water, watching it skip the surface twice before sinking.

Two skips? Pfft, I can do better than that!

I root around for another pebble—flatter the better—while humming the melody for "Looking for love in all the wrong places," thumbing the stone in my hand before releasing it to the water. It skids beautifully, skips four times, then sinks.

Nice one, Halbrook!

I skip rocks for at least twenty minutes, hunting on the ground for the perfect stones then watching as they hop, jump, and sink, trying to beat my best score.

Not that it's a competition.

Can't be if I'm the only one playing.

I check the time, confident Thad and Mia will be done doing whatever it is they've been doing the past half hour *cough, banging* and make my way back up the trail, so we can get this day started and kick it in the rear.

Plus, we have reservations in a few for a tour of the lake on a pontoon boat, and I'd hate to be late.

I find everyone on the small porch of the camper I'm sharing with Juliet, the three of them laughing when I walk up.

"You done going to the bathroom?" I ask my roommate, giving her a commiserating nudge with my elbow. "Everything come out okay?"

She blanches, but manages to roll her pretty blue eyes, nudging me back. "Everything is fine, thanks."

"Cool." I focus my attention on Thad. "Boat should be here to grab us any minute—we should head back down there."

Thad cocks his head thoughtfully. "I thought we were going fishing today instead—pontoon cruise tomorrow at sunset."

Shit, I think he might be right. "Come to think of it, I did see a guy down there loading up a boat. Must have been ours."

Mia's long, black lashes flutter. "I love fishing."

Juliet looks at her. "You do?" The 'since when' remains unspoken, but lingers in the air, the only oblivious one is Thad.

"Obviously," Mia laughs. "My dad always used to take me when I was a kid. It's been a while but I love it so much."

Thad takes her hand and kisses it. "Beautiful *and* outdoorsy."

Holding hands, they head down the path toward the water.

"Outdoorsy?" Juliet mutters. "Is he high?"

"High on love," I grin, dragging her along. "How about you? Do you fish?"

She considers this question and as she does, I steal furtive glances at her.

Baseball cap with her ponytail pulled through the back. Glossy lips, but otherwise, no other makeup. Freckles across her perky nose. Hoop earrings.

Jeans and sweatshirt.

Dang she's cute for someone so suspicious.

"I've only been fishing a few times in my life. Never really had the opportunity, my dad wasn't into it. My grandpa was, but I grew up in Illinois and my grandparents lived in Arizona, so I didn't see them often and in Arizona, there aren't many places with bodies of water." She pauses, following next to me down the trail. "Is that all he cares about? Her looks?"

"Who, Thad? Uh—no. He's not superficial at all." Okay, that may not be entirely true. Clearly Mia is drop-dead gorgeous, so that was the first thing that attracted him to her. But she's funny and sweet and those are the things that keep him attracted to her.

"Whatever you say."

She does not sound convinced.

"Thad and I are sapiosexuals—we recently discovered this after too many bottles of beer, while paying close attention to the halftime commercial during a football game on one of Thad's bye weeks. One came on for an online dating app, ergo, we're sapiosexuals."

That's how I know Thad likes Mia for Mia, and not because Mia looks like a model.

Er.

Yeah.

"A sapio-what now?"

"Sapiosexual. Finding someone's mind to be the most attractive thing about them over physical appearances."

Juliet snorts. "Oh yeah? Then why has he been photographed with actresses and models if he's so attracted to brains?"

I laugh, amused. "Please. Don't believe everything you see online."

She is still not convinced and *how did this trail become so damn long*? Are we there yet?

"Don't believe everything I see or read online? How can you say that when he's photographed with a beautiful new someone every single week?"

"It's part of the job."

She snorts again. "Uh, okay."

"Did a bug fly up your nose? Why do you keep snorting?"

She waves a hand aimlessly. "It's just something I unintentionally do, okay? I inherited the snort gene from my mother."

"Genetic snorting?"

"Yes."

"Hey." I touch her arm to stop her before we're down on the shore, within hearing distance of Thad and Mia. "I was being serious—before Thad met Mia, part of his job was to pretend to be dating certain people. Publicists set it up, it's basically publicity stunts, more so, for the actresses and models. Helps everyone out."

"How does that help out a football player?"

"Because, the more fans and public love him, the more visible he is on social media, the more companies want to endorse him." Long story short? Money."

She's silent. Then, "Oh. I guess that makes sense."

We continue walking. "And for the record, some of those gorgeous women you've seen were his sisters. He brings them to events a lot and they are stunning."

"Models too, no doubt."

"No. Keelee is a fifth grade teacher who happens to be married, and Victoria is getting her master's. He's brought both of them to the ESPY's a few times, but mostly, his agent sets up photo ops with female celebrities to boost his popularity. Happens all the time."

"Interesting."

"Yeah—so don't be thinking he's a scumbag skirt chaser. He's not."

Juliet seems to take my word on this as we finally arrive at the fishing boat that's been pulled up to the shore, fishing poles sticking out in their holders, the guide already in the driver seat. I don't remember hiring one—both Thad and I know a thing or two about how to drive a boat, and with four adults in the small space? It sure would be a tight fit if the dude stays.

He's as big as we are.

I notice a large wicker picnic basket and a big beverage cooler taking up additional precious space; one more body just isn't going to work, even if someone is going to use the cooler as seating.

"Hey, Captain?" I greet the guy. "I don't think we hired a guide for the day? Tomorrow night we have someone driving the sunset cruise, but today, I believe we are on our own?" I don't want to come off as a complete asshole, so I pose it as a question.

"That right?" The dude takes off his ballcap and scratches his chin. "Fine by me. I'll just pull her up to the dock, so you can all safely board and if you aren't needin' me today, I can come back in a few hours." He waits while Thad and I deliberate.

"Yeah buddy, I think we're good. I've been driving about half my life." My buddy digs in his back pocket and produces his wallet, peeling it open and shelling out a few bills.

Not wanting to look like a schmuck, I do the same.

"Thanks for your time, bro, appreciate it. We'll circle back around at the end of the day."

Can we pause to mention that Thad is sponsored by a wildlife and outdoor supply company? Yeah, he does do the scout and fishing guide thing more often than not, but I think today he was looking forward to some privacy with Mia.

Pretty lake. Pretty girl.

Picnic lunch.

Quiet setting, beautiful weather.

Kind of romantic in a way.

The guy wants to flirt with his girlfriend and show off a little bit—can't quite do that with a professional in the boat giving you instructions you're already familiar with, can you?

Don't blame him for tipping the guy and sending him on his merry way.

"Cell service should be good, I'll shoot you my number."

Now my best friend is scratching at *his* chin in thought. "How about we call it three o'clock—don't want to be out terribly long, the girls may get bored."

"Three o'clock?" Mia gulps. "That's like..." I can see her mentally counting the hours being trapped in a fishing boat, her eyes darting from us to the boat. "Four hours."

"I brought a book," Juliet perkily announces, pulling it out of the back of her pants. She's had it tucked into her waist-band, grinning with the announcement.

Her friend groans. "Ugh, why didn't I think of that?"

Juliet loops her arm through her friend's. "You can

41

sunbathe on that little sundeck thingy if you get bored. It'll be the perfect weather for it."

Sundeck thingy?

I think she's referring to the bow, where the trolling motor is situated and where we can stand to cast.

But sundeck thingy works, too, I guess.

"Oh, good idea!"

The guide gets us all situated, showing us the bait, the rods, and giving us a quick overview of the control panels. Where everything is stored, safety features, life jackets and cushions, the whole shebang, before sending us on our way.

Off we go!

CHAPTER 3

Juliet

F ishing sucks.

Correction: I suck at fishing.

Fumbling with yet another worm (I refuse to use a leech as bait), I hold in a sour expression as the guts ooze out of it when I wrap it around the hook, listening as Thad coaches Mia on how to do it.

I copy the instructions, mimicking her movements—the only thing that isn't the same is a strong pair of masculine arms wrapped around me as I complete the task.

Not that I care.

Pfft.

Nearby, Davis sits in the front—they've popped a chair up on the sundeck, or bow or whatever they insist on calling it (as if it were a yacht), so he can get a clear view of the water below, and at the same time lob back playful insults at his best friend.

They're cute—much as I hate to admit it.

And Thad isn't the worst, much as I hate to admit that, too. He seems genuinely interested in Mia and her happiness, doing his best to fuss over her while we're out here on the water, baiting her hook and handing her the water bottle.

He even insisted she apply sunscreen, twice.

"You should do that, too, you know," Davis had told me, *butting into my business.*

"Do what?"

"Put on sunscreen. You have really fair skin, you don't want to burn it."

I'd glanced up at the sun; it wasn't hot, but it was warm, no cover or shade to hide behind—just this baseball cap to protect my skin.

"Fine." Our fingers had brushed when he'd handed me the bottle and I'd shivered. Shivered, if you can believe it, for a guy that doesn't even give me a lady boner!

I finally get the worm on my hook and pull back on the rod, holding it the way I'd been shown earlier, grasping it so just my thumb is on the reel, ready to release the bail.

I've cast the line a few times already—not that I've been overly successful at it. The line hasn't gone out farther than fifteen feet—but practice makes perfect, and I am determined to impress my friends.

Determined to impress Davis.

I'm seated in the back of the boat, directly behind Davis, while Mia and Thad sit to my right, both blissfully unaware that I am attempting to maneuver my line. Blissfully unaware of the danger they're in from my hook.

Paying close attention so that I don't whack either of them with the rod, I repeat what I'd been told, uttering them as I go along. "Pull the rod tip back so the tip sweeps over your dominant shoulder. Then bring it forward swiftly and point the rod tip at your target."

My target: the water.

This I can do—I'm literally surrounded by it, so what does it even matter where I aim it?

I release the line with my finger, the weight of the lure pulls the line off the reel, and truly: *this is my worst nightmare.*

Off the line goes.

My eyes scan the water, waiting for the plop and ripple the hook and bait should be making...any...second now...

"Fuck!" comes a loud, girly shout.

Thad jumps up out of his seat, falling toward the front of the boat and Davis, who is holding his lip.

"Don't move! Juliet, don't move."

"What's happening, babe?" Mia cranes her neck to see the action while I scan the water for my lure, twisting my body and the rod to the left.

"Mothereffer!" Another frantic shout from Davis and I shoot up, out of my seat.

"Oh my god, Juliet, you've hooked him in the freaking head!"

"What? No, I..." My head whips around, eyes frantically following the line of vision—not into the water, but to Davis's ear, blood already trickling down his neck.

No.

No, no, no, no—this cannot be happening.

"Oh my god!" I cry, embarrassed and horrified. "Oh my god."

My first reaction is to toss the fishing pole onto the floor of the boat, quickly remembering the end of it is latched onto a man's face.

Holy shit, holy shit, holy shit!

"Everyone calm down," Thad instructs. "It didn't go deep. Luckily she's not great at casting."

I would be insulted, but alas, my efforts did result in a sharp hook latching itself into a man's face. Ear. Almost his lip.

"It didn't go deep," Davis laughs. "That's what she said."

"Really, bro? You're bleeding out of your skull and you've got jokes?"

"I'm hooked by the ear, not bleeding out my ass."

45

I catch his barb in time for our eyes to meet while Thad uses pliers to snap the line so he can release his friend, Davis's eyes widening as he cringes.

"Just pull it out, dude," he tells his friend.

"I can't. I might throw up."

"Thad, just do it."

"You know how I get around blood."

"Seriously—I don't want to sit around with this thing stuck in my ear. Just pull it out, it'll be fine."

"Halbrook, remember the time I—"

"Oh my god—I'll do it." I caused this mess, I will fix it.

Plus, I'm no stranger to the occasional bleeding appendages—I once took cooking classes at Le Cordon Bleu and you'd be shocked at how many culinary students almost chop their fingers off.

"Are you sure?" Thad asks as I climb carefully to Davis at the front of the boat, he's still planted in his seat, ramrod straight. "Do you want the first aid kit?"

"Yeah, you should probably look to see if there's any astringent in there. Maybe a bandage or something?"

Mia springs into action to retrieve it while I crouch in front of Davis to get a good look at his lobe.

I cringe. "I really got you good."

My ill attempt at a joke is met with another cringe.

"Right. Okay then—I'll be serious."

I paste on a serious expression, so that no one thinks I'm too blasé about this, or that I'm not taking this seriously. I quite literally hooked a guy—not the way I wanted to reel one in, but I suppose I'll take what I can get.

Ha ha, *kidding*.

Mia hands me the first aid kit and I inspect Davis's injury without touching it; the last thing I wanna do is hurt him before I start removing it. The skin is tender and raw and bleeding—but not as much blood as I thought there would be.

It was hard to tell from where I was sitting how bad this was. Not the worst, thank goodness.

"Okay," I say. "Hold still."

"Thanks, I knew that already," Davis says wryly.

I resist the urge to roll my eyes at him; he's in a vulnerable state.

One that *I* created.

Gingerly, I touch the hook—it's not all the way in, basically just a few millimeters or so. Nothing life threatening. Nothing he'll need medical attention for.

Easy peasy.

I brace myself. "This might hurt."

"It already does," he says impatiently. "Just yank it out."

"I'm not going to *yank* it." Give me some credit, dude.

"The suspense is killing me more than the pain is," he informs me. "Do it."

"Stop pushing, I'll get to it."

I swear a bead of sweat forms on my brow, and I pray more beadlettes don't join in on the party. The last thing I want is to perspire on the poor guy.

Davis sighs. "Any day now."

And here I thought he was a patient man.

Or maybe that's just when he doesn't have tiny knives spearing his body.

"Okay," I say again, for lack of anything else to say. "Here I go."

Licking my lips, I brace myself—more so for his sake than for mine; this obviously isn't going to hurt me in the least.

One.

Two.

Two and a half...

"Fuck!" Davis breathes, cursing for the third time when I lift out the silver hook with a firm tug, blood spilling out and Mia steps in with a swab, already dabbing.

"Shit, sorry for swearing again, but that hurt."

"It's fine—I don't blame you." I add, "I'm sorry too. I don't actually know what I'm doing as far as fishing goes and probably shouldn't have been casting my own line."

Davis lets out a puff of air. "I survived and now we have a story to tell."

When Davis smiles—pearly white and beaming—I take a step back, almost falling off the ledge with a gasp as he reaches out to catch my hand and pull me back with lightning speed.

"Still have those mad quick reflexes I see," Thad laughs. "Damn, bro." He's there with an assist, righting me, so I don't topple ass over tea kettle onto the floor of the boat.

I sit my ass down, parking it in my spot and not moving a muscle. "I'm going to stay here and not move, so I don't harm or maim anyone else."

"The entire last ten minutes killed my buzz," Davis adds, winking at me when we lock eyes again.

Dammit! Stop looking at him!

I can't help it, he's right there!

Not to mention—really good-looking.

That's the first time—and the last time—I'm going to admit that to myself, locking the information away so I can keep my distance and not fall under his spell.

Handsome guys like this are trouble, and I don't know of a single one who could be faithful.

I don't know a whole lot about Davis's history but I do know he played professional ball, too, which can only mean he's had his fair share of one-night stands and sleeping his way through every city they played in.

Don't hate the player...

It's hard to, honestly.

Davis is...

Ugh.

Decent.

I don't *hate* him, but I'm going to do my best to be as leery as I am around Thad, keeping my brain and hormones in check as Mia should have been doing the night she met Thad and invited him back to her condo.

Killer grin.

Great body.

Easygoing.

What's not to like?

Nothing. You like nothing, you are not going to date him, you are not going to like him. End of story, period point blank.

Let's be real: any woman with a functioning set of eyes would notice how attractive either of these gentlemen are. And it's not a *crime* to look, is it?

I mean, it's either him or the clouds in the sky, or the lake, or the trees.

As the two guys pack up our stuff and pull the boat's anchor out of the water, I mull over what my actual type is. Mull over what type of man would catch my eye in the wild, if I were looking for love.

It's been a while since I've had a boyfriend and even longer since I've taken the search seriously; people think that meeting someone is a breeze, especially when you're a funny, successful, and smart woman—but the ugly truth is, it's not.

Not in the least.

Do you know how many bad dates I've been on with guys who completely misrepresented themselves on the dating apps? Dozens.

One single guy was married—the Married Single, we call that.

One guy drank twelve cocktails in an hour—TWELVE.

I had to call him a car.

Another? Told me he wasn't interested in dating, he was

just seeing what was out there—but if I wanted to have sex with him, that was cool, too.

Waste.

Of.

Time.

Dozens of wasted nights and hours and calories from meals I hadn't wanted to eat in the first place and drinks I hadn't wanted to drink when I could've stayed home on my couch instead.

In my wiener dog pajamas.

My eyes stray to Davis as Thad roars the engine to life, steering us back toward the shore, and I watch as he touches his bandaged-up ear every so often, his hair blowing in the breeze, sunglasses shielding his eyes.

It seems he hasn't shaved in days, but that doesn't detract from the goodness of his bone structure; square jaw and beautiful lips. *Bet he's smooth talked his way into plenty of panties with that mouth...*

I scowl, eyes looking away.

Mia is watching me with a smirk on her face.

"What?"

She shrugs. "Nothing."

"I can't look in that direction?"

Now she laughs. "I didn't say anything."

She didn't say anything with her mouth, but she's saying it with her eyes, and I'm here to tell her, "Don't be a shit. I am taking in my view."

"I'd say you were."

"Not that view. The trees and the lake."

The engine whirs us closer to shore and as soon as we dock, I'm up and out of my seat, ready to climb out for land with Mia at my side.

While Thad and Davis handle the boat—the guide is back and going over logistics with them—my best friend and I walk back to camp, my stomach already growling.

"I'm going to take a nap," Mia says with a yawn.

"Do you actually mean you're going to take a nap, or do you mean *nap* nap?"

She wiggles her eyebrows with a laugh. "Depends on Thad, I guess."

"Okay, so not a nap."

"Probably not an actual nap—but I'll try until he comes back." She stops in front of my cute little camper. "They're serving snacks I think—boxes they're bringing to each camper, isn't that cute?"

So cute.

"And I think dinner is at six, then they're doing a bonfire tonight."

"Oh, I love that! With s'mores?"

"I think so. It will be fun meeting everyone who arrived this morning."

She hugs me before heading back to her tent and I manage to sneak inside my camper before Davis returns, closing the door to the tiny bedroom and flipping its little lock—climb onto the bed and pass out.

———

WHY IS IT DARK OUT?

I stir, blinking back the dark, raising my head to glance around, unable to see anything at all.

Where am I?

Why is it so damn dark out?

I just closed my eyes for a second, I couldn't have slept the night away?

Moving my arm so I can see my watch, I poke at it to reveal the time.

Eight o'clock!

I slept the entire afternoon and no one came to wake me? What kind of shit is that? What about dinner? What about the bonfire?

I peek through the window in the camper's bedroom and see the glow of a fire in the near distance slightly down the shore a bit, and people sitting around it.

My stomach growls and as I sit up, I can't help but wonder if there will be food around the campfire—I am a girl who never misses a meal and I don't want to start tonight.

Since I have zero things packed for a bonfire, I throw on the same sweatshirt I had on earlier today, keep on the jeans I'm wearing, and add sneakers. Hair still in a pony, I push gold hoops through my ears.

Hey, we may be in the wilderness, but that's no reason not to accessorize!

It's a bit creepy meandering through the campers in the dark, but I make my way, following the fire, and arrive to loud chattering and plenty of laughter.

New faces.

Friendly faces.

Everyone spots me at the same time, and Mia waves, pointing to an empty seat beside her. Beside that chair? Davis.

I run a hand through my ponytail and walk taller, pasting on a tired smile.

"Where have you been?" Mia hisses in a hushed tone as I drop into the lawn chair.

"Sleeping. Why didn't anyone wake me up?" I glance over at my roommate. "I could have been dead in that bedroom, you should have woken me up."

"I tried. I banged on the door."

He did? "I didn't hear any knocking."

"First I knocked, then I banged—just figured you were exhausted from all the excitement this morning." He hands me a glass filled with a yellowish liquid. "Here. Lionel made this—it's homemade spirits."

Spirits. Does he mean moonshine?

And who is Lionel?

I take the glass and eye it skeptically.

Give it a sniff. "What is this?"

"Try a sip, it's good. I barely feel my ear throbbing anymore."

I cringe and look around him, trying to get a view of his ear. "I'm so sorry—does it hurt?"

Tentatively, I sip from the glass of liquor—scrunching up my face from the taste. It reeks like gasoline and tastes like it, too.

"Yeah it hurts, but I took a pain reliever and this booze helps." He lifts his glass and sips from it. "Let me introduce you around, everyone has been waiting patiently for you to rise from your slumber." Davis clears his throat and begins making introductions to a group of people I haven't met before. "Hey everyone, we have a newcomer! Sleeping Beauty here has decided to grace us with her presence."

I bristle at the term Sleeping Beauty, but paste on a smile —a groggy smile—and raise a hand in a wave. "Hi. I'm Juliet."

"Hi, Juliet," comes a chorus of voices, some of them most definitely drunk.

"Juliet," Davis says, pointing across the firepit. "That is Erik and Cookie—they're from Baltimore."

Cookie simpers while Erik waves at me again. They're holding hands and drinking beer with big grins on their faces —some would liken those smiles to the Cheshire Cat smile, but I just woke up from a long nap, so what do I know?

"And that's Lionel and his wife Suzanne." They nod at me. "Ken and the other Suzanne."

"The Other Suzanne," the other Suzanne giggles. "I love that."

Everyone laughs.

"And Steve and Paul are from Chicago," Davis continues, indicating another couple across the way.

Everyone seems like they're having a great time, and it appears as though Mia and Thad are lost in their own world as Mia roasts two fluffy marshmallows on a stick, rotating it around and around, so it cooks evenly.

Yum.

I glance around to see if there is any other food available besides marshmallows, chocolate and graham crackers, delighted to spy a big basket brimming with campfire treats.

Rising, I go to the basket set on a picnic table that's been pulled closer to the action and used as a buffet table, and gather up the ingredients for a pudgy pie: bread, spread on Nutella and raspberry jam—then take it over to the fire where the square pie iron is resting on a log.

Hunched over like a troll, I bake my little pie, excited at the notion of campfire food despite myself. Do I wish I'd woken up and had a proper meal? Sure. Does that make me less excited to be eating chocolate for dinner because I skipped dinner?

A bit.

Someone could have woken me up—it would have been the thoughtful thing to do.

Hmph.

I can't live on chocolate alone, though some people do try.

My pie cooks and simmers.

For an eternity, it seems.

No rush, pie—don't mind me, I'm only starving to death.

I tip back and sip from the horrid moonshine, the fire in my belly casting some of my hunger away—and after a few minutes, I decide the chocolate sandwich needn't be completely cooked through and the bread doesn't need to be crisp; after all, it's a sandwich that doesn't contain meat.

I pull open the cast iron by the handle; from out of nowhere, Davis comes in with the assist, taking it from me and handing me a plate I'd forgotten to grab.

I shoot him a grateful look, my ooey gooey goodness steaming with heat, smoldering and delicious.

I moan before it hits my lips. Tempted, but not stupid; if I take a bite now, it'll likely burn off my tastebuds and then where will I be? Sad and still hungry.

More moonshine hits my tongue.

The fire in my belly gets weaker as I get used to the flavor and taste and smell.

"Who made this again?" I ask, voice louder than it needs to be. Even I'm aware of that but let's be real: I'm buzzed after a few sips. I'm also aware that I've already been told who made it, but, again...buzzed brain.

Well-rested and loopy.

"Lionel brought it with him. Made it himself."

"Tastes like gasoline and shattered dreams." Still, that doesn't stop me from drinking more of it. "My pudgy pie will make it taste better though."

Taking a bite, I already know before it hits my lips I'm going to love it—and I do. The hazelnut spread oozes from every side, jam along with it, bread slightly crusted and delightful.

I wash it down with another tiny sip of Lionel's magic juice. "Damn that's tasty."

Davis eyeballs the glass warily. "Er. Maybe you should have water, too."

Eh. Why drink water when this gutter juice is starting to taste so darn delicious? "Maybe I should make a s'more once I'm done with this sammy."

"Maybe you should have twenty sammies—you need actual food." Davis disappears while I'm eating the last of my cute, tasty, treat, offering me a croissant. "Here. Better eat some heartier carbs."

Hearty carbs?

What is that even?

"This would be amazing dipped in chocolate," I muse as I nibble at the end, inspecting it before it goes into my mouth. Sip on the liquor. Nibble more bread.

The fire crackles and pops as guests roast marshmallows and laugh and drink, and eventually, I plop back down in my chair to listen to the chatter.

"Davis, tell us," the woman named Cookie says from across the fire. "How is it that a man like you is single?"

Well.

"That was rude," I mutter beside him, more to myself than him, feeling good in the neighborhood and edgy on his behalf. Not that it's any of my business—I don't know the guy and have spent all of one hour with him, half of that time was spent digging a hook out of his earlobe.

It was a fine earlobe, but still.

Davis chuckles, but even with liquor inside me I can tell it's strained. "Just haven't found the right one."

"So. No dating?"

He hesitates. "Yes, I date. Sort of."

"What does that mean? *Sort* of?" The Other Suzanne chimes in. She seems as buzzed as I'm feeling.

I watch the exchange while chomping on the croissant I'd been given, sincerely wishing it was smothered in something sweet.

S'more.

A s'more croissant sounds absolutely yummy.

The Other Suzanne looks like the kind of woman who loves to gossip, drinks too much, and flirts with other men relentlessly—same as Cookie, though she's way more blatant about it.

I wonder if they're swingers...

I ponder this idea as I load a metal stick with marshmallows, prepared to cook three at a time; one to eat on its own, two for the graham cracker sammich.

"Have you always been single?" the women ask, almost in tandem, the question irritating me to no end.

"Nope, he hasn't," Thad chimes in, feet extended in front of him as he sits in his chair lazily. I get the feeling he doesn't want to be left out of the conversation and thinks it's his duty to give them information on his friend. "Had a few steady girlfriends. Horrible people who weren't right for him. Not like my sweet cheeks here."

Mia blushes in the moonlight.

"The longest relationship I have had is with the ladies at the Humane Society," Davis laughs, poking the fire with a fire iron that he retrieved from the ground and digging into the embers, stoking it.

"Ladies at the Humane Society?" I blurt out, interested, but not wanting to be interested.

Yes, I'm purposely trying not to like this man; I know it's wrong and I know I shouldn't have decided before I got here that I wasn't going to like him—that doesn't stop me from being a grouch.

Regardless, it suddenly strikes me that I may have prejudged him based on my own past experiences. Don't we all do that though? Aren't we all guilty of doing that?

Is it his fault that I dated a string of good-looking, successful guys who ended up betraying me? Is it his fault that my last boyfriend—a semi-professional baseball player—slept with a woman who used to hang around the ball park after the games?

Davis used to be a professional athlete—I cannot imagine how many gold diggers used to sniff around him. Cannot imagine a man that funny and good-looking being faithful.

Bah humbug!

I chuckle at my own reference to Christmas—my favorite holiday of the year—which makes no sense and is so super random of an insertion into my brain.

Insertion.

Picturing a penis going into a vagina has me giggling again like a fifteen-year-old boy, despite the fact that no one here can hear my brain to be in on my joke. Oh god, I must be drunk! It must be this moonshine—*I have to stop drinking it.*

No more drinks, Juliet, put the glass down!

But it's so good!

No, Juliet, it's really not. It's garbage. You like it because you're drunk-ish, not because it tastes good. You're a wine snob, not a moonshine girl, get it together.

When in Rome!

I glance around—everyone around the fire pit seems to be drinking the same liquid, barring a few dudes drinking beer, Thad included.

Narrowing my eyes, I watch him smile at Mia, the ice around my heart melting—so far, he hasn't been the horrible piece of crap I'd assumed he was. Then again, the only women around this weekend are older, middle-aged women with partners.

Still, he's been attentive, funny and okay—seems to really genuinely love my bestie, and if what Davis says is true—that he's only been seen out with socialites and movie stars for the sake of publicity and popularity...guess I can't fault him for that. Not if he's being paid and all to chaperone and smile for the cameras.

Can't fault the dude for trying to keep his career game strong.

Maybe I should give the guy a break, and give Mia some credit: she's not dated as many losers as I have. Her picker seems to be way better than mine.

A hiccup escapes my lips as my eyes go to Erik and Cookie; they're eyeing up Davis, head together while they chat, eye fucking him if I'd ever seen anyone eye fuck.

Eyes, eyes, eyes.

I burp, covering my mouth with a giggle, marshmallow on my hands getting in my hair.

Drat. I'm making a sticky mess.

Totally forgot I had one in my hand, I move to load the stick with more marshmallows, watching the fire crackle and pop as I rotate my hand to get an even roast, wondering if I should start the entire thing on fire to speed up the process.

Crackle.

Pop.

Vaguely, I listen to the voices around me, and turn my head when Mia begins repeating my name. "Are you listening? Thad just asked if the s'more tasted good."

I lift my head to stare at her boyfriend, a giant among men who's waiting for my answer as if it means something to him.

"It's good—yummy. I'm going to eat another one I think." I pause, deciding that he's doing his best to be inclusive and not ignore me. "What about you? Have you tried some?"

Another hiccup escapes my mouth, causing them to glance at each other.

"I'm allergic to chocolate, but I have had a few marshmallows," Thad says—much to my horror.

"Allergic to chocolate?" I damn near hop out of my chair, aghast at the idea someone can't eat chocolate for the sake of their health. "What does that even mean?"

He needs to explain it, slowly, in terms I can understand. A life without chocolate? What kind of life is that?

"Don't know; just can't eat it, otherwise I blow up like a puffer fish."

"Realllyyy." I lean toward him, fascinated. "I'm not

allergic to anything. Once I ate almost an entire flat of strawberries after we went and picked them and got a rash all over my body, but that was an isolated incident."

Thad laughs, his pearly, chemically whitened teeth shine in the firelight.

He is very handsome; guess I haven't actually given him a thorough once-over before, not wanting to eyeball my best friend's boyfriend. I'd die if she ever got the impression I was into him, so I never look directly at him.

Is that weird?

Okay fine—it *is* a little weird; but you get the reason I do it. The last thing I want is to be one of those women who drool out the side of my mouth because I'm judging his good looks the same way everyone else does.

So you judge him by the things you've read about him online or seen on television? That's not cool either, Juliet.

Um, hello—could my inner voices please quiet themselves while I'm having a moment here?

Sheesh.

I peer into my near empty glass. "Who made this juice again?"

"It's not juice, Juliet—it's liquor. Lionel made it, remember?" Mia laughs, pointing to the man across the fire. Upon further inspection, I notice he has gray hair and a ponytail, the sort of dude you'd expect to be making moonshine, but probably as a hobby.

Lionel looks affluent, if one can look affluent while wearing plaid and torn up jeans.

He salutes us, raising his glass, smiling through his Santalike beard.

"It tastes like shit, so why do I like it?"

"Because you're drunk," Mia states wryly, a half-smile on her pretty face. She pats me on the head. "There there, you should slow down."

"Or eat more food," Davis chimes in, handing me the pack of graham crackers and pulling out two. "Here, nibble on these."

I follow the directions—not because I want him bossing me around, but because I happen to like graham crackers and know I need to eat.

"Can you whip me up another mallow?" I've only eaten eight, and who's counting if I eat a few more? "Please?"

Davis obliges, kneeling near the fire with my abandoned roasting stick, lighting two marshmallows on fire. We all watch them burn to a crisp, my mouth watering with anticipation at the gooey center that's surely inside.

And why I'm getting so amped up over all this junk food is beyond me. I should be ashamed of myself for sleeping through an actual meal and pounding down sugar.

I'll never be able to sleep tonight!

I feel Davis's presence beside me each and every time he moves or shifts in his seat—and when our fingers touch as he gives me the melted treats, I tingle a little bit in my girly parts despite myself. There's nothing special about this person, I don't even know him—so why do I keep having these little reactions to him over nothing?

The rest of the guests continue chatting and laughing.

"Davis," Lionel directs the conversation toward him. "What is it you do now that you're not playing ball?"

Davis is handing me marshmallows, and I painstakingly and drunkenly nestle them between two graham crackers with a bit of chocolate, creating a tiny bed of deliciousness.

Yummy yum yum.

"I'm in finance now." He licks the melted mallow from his fingers. "Most of my clients are professional athletes." He pauses for a few seconds. "I also do a bit of volunteering. Animal shelters and a lot during the holidays, mostly for children in need."

Animal rescue? Working with children?

Did my ovaries just explode, or is this just my drunk self reacting?

"What do you do when you volunteer at the shelter?" Lionel's wife, Suzanne, asks with a bit of a slur. Everyone is having a great time, drinking her husband's concoction and other libations.

"I help find foster homes for animals, and I don't know, shovel shit out of kennels and snuggle the cats." He shrugs good-naturedly. "Whatever I can do to lend a hand. I really want a dog but I used to be gone a lot and the partners I've had in the past weren't really...animal lovers."

Suzanne tips her head. "Not animal lovers? What does that mean?"

"You know—they cared more about themselves than other people and didn't want pets around. The hair and," Davis shifts uncomfortably in his seat while I listen, riveted. This is all very good information. "You know how some people want all the attention?"

Everyone nods, campfire casting shadows on everyone's somber faces as Davis weaves his tale.

"Those are the women I've dated in the past and all I wanted was a cute place with a yard and a damn dog or two."

Cute place with a yard? What does that mean?

"So you dated superficial women who cared about looks and not much else," the other Suzanne sums up what we're all thinking.

"In my defense," Davis begins. "It's real hard to know what someone's intentions are until you've been with them awhile. It's easy to fake it and pretend you're something you're not when you're only seeing that person once a week or every few weeks."

"When do the real colors begin to show?"

"When they start leaving shit at your condo and staying over more—that reveals a lot."

"Preach!" Thad chimes in, putting his arm around Mia. "Been there, done that. It may seem like glitz and glamour in the spotlight, but it's not easy finding genuine connections." He kisses Mia on the temple. "So many users out there."

"What about dating all those celebrities?" my drunk self can't stop from asking.

Hey, I'm here to learn more about the guy, right? I wouldn't be doing my job as Mia's bestie if I let this opportunity slide.

"You know the saying, 'Don't believe everything you read?' Well these days, it's 'Don't believe everything you see online.' Lots of those dates were arranged and I had never met the women before and never saw them again after that night. Lots of movie premiers and shit—get paid to do those."

He's mentioned that before.

"Really? You get paid to go to movie premiers?" I can't help, but ask, even though Davis told me pretty much this exact same thing this morning. However, I don't trust easily and I want to hear it from Thad's mouth. Ease the last of my worries.

"Sure. And appearances, get paid to do those too. Night clubs and shit will shell out a lot of money to have athletes and celebs there to draw in a bigger crowd."

"How much?" Paul can't stop from blurting out. His partner Steve elbows him in the ribs.

Thad laughs and demurs. "Depends. Some A-listers get one, two-hundred thousand just to show up for an hour. It's crazy, man."

Davis nods. "It sure is."

"And you know." Thad is musing. "When that's your life —when you're paid to club, or go to shows, or to appear in public—you're not meeting authentic people, you're meeting fans. So try finding a girlfriend in that crowd who wants an actual future with you..."

"...not just their bills paid," Davis finishes for him and they toast, clinking their glass and beer can together.

"Amen, my friend."

Thad gazes across the fire. "How did y'all meet?"

Lionel and Suzanne are the first to answer. "Online. That Silver Singles app. Never thought I'd meet a man who likes Christmas as much as I do."

Lionel chuckles. "She loves when I dress up as Santa."

Oh jeez. I didn't need that visual.

"We met online, too," Paul responds. "He was the first date I'd been on after a five-month dry-spell."

"What are the odds it would have been a love match?" Mia swoons.

"Are we the only ones who met in a bar?" Cookie giggles, nudging Erik. "Say it isn't so!"

"Now, now, it was a bar at a fancy restaurant we met at and she was there with a group of girlfriends; I was there for a business meeting—let's not paint a picture like we were in a pool hall." Erik fake laughs, downplaying his wife's story.

"True, but still—it was at the bar." Cookie shrugs.

"Did he buy you a drink?" Suzanne asks.

"He bought all my girlfriends a drink and paid for our dinner."

"La di dah!" Suzanne croons. "Ken and I met on a blind date our friends set us up on. His friend Brent and my cousin Neely played matchmaker. We'll be celebrating our twentieth anniversary next month."

All around the fire we make a show of being impressed. "What are you going to do to celebrate?"

"We're taking our kids on a cruise," Ken deadpans. "I'm sure it'll be dramatic and miserable."

"Ken!" Suzanne laughs. "Stop it."

"What! You know I'm right. Alex and Paige will fight the whole time and Erin will cry that we didn't bring her boyfriend."

Suzanne's expression is one of chagrin. "Yeah, he's probably right."

"I am right and I'm already exhausted."

Everyone laughs.

I swallow the rest of the moonshine in my glass and stare through the side at the emptiness.

Sigh.

"How about you, Thad? You and your lady haven't told us how you met."

"Well." Thad puts his giant paw on my friend's leg. "Why don't you tell the story, babe."

Babe.

Ugh.

I want to be someone's Babe.

"He was in line behind me at Starbucks getting coffee, and my app wasn't loading and I hadn't brought my wallet in, so he let them zap his app and paid for my drink."

Awww, of course, I've heard this already, but I love watching her face when she tells it.

The crowd goes wild.

I do love the story of how they met—how my best friend always loves going inside the coffee shop instead of the drive-thru, despite how busy it might be or how inconvenient the location. Mia is the world's last sweetheart who cherishes small moments—like clutching a warm coffee cup in her cold hands on a rainy morning before work.

She loves painting and listening to music and stopping to pet animals when she's taking her afternoon walk.

I don't blame Thad one bit for falling head over heels in love with her from the moment they met—she is adorable.

"And when he paid for my drink I couldn't thank him enough—"

"—You would have thought I'd bought her a new car or something," he laughs, kissing her again. "She's so cute. I had to get her number. Never let an opportunity pass you by."

They finish each other sentences.

Now all eyes turn to Davis and I—the only two single people amongst us. If they think they're going to get a story out of either of us, they are sadly mistaken; we're obviously not a couple, but it feels weird to over explain that we are two strangers who just met who happen to be sharing a cabin.

"What about the two of you?" Paul inevitably asks. He's a nosy little bugger.

"Juliet and I are here for moral support." Davis grins. "Got to keep an eye on these two, make sure they're not getting into any trouble. Plus, we're all here in the woods, right? Trying to relax. Besides, big guy here needs someone to bait his hook."

He most certainly did not bait Thad's hook, and I half expect him to mention his torn-up ear.

"So you're *not* a couple?" Cookie wants clarification. "You sure do look cute together."

Well duh. I'm cute and he's handsome and we both have brown hair.

We match.

Davis is shaking his head. "No, no—nothing like that."

I'm glad he's not vehemently denying we're together in a way that's insulting—that would make me feel shitty even though we are not together, if that makes sense?

"Well, you have a few more days trapped in that little cottage—anything can happen," I vaguely hear Cookie say.

Do the trees look like they're swaying? The one on the left looks like a dinosaur. Wait, no—a mountain range.

Is that a mountain range? Shit. Are we that far west?

I've never been good at geography, the hell if I know where we're even at.

We could be murdered and I wouldn't know where to send the ambulance!

I giggle.

Nibble on more crackers like Davis told me to. "God these are good."

Famous.

Last.

Words.

CHAPTER 4

Davis

"Oh my god, I want to die."

We haven't even made it as far as the camper when Juliet announces she's dizzy and I wouldn't be surprised if she throws up.

She wavers on our walk, the rest of the group separating for the night, disappearing into the dark night, so I take her arm and guide her along the path. It's lit, but not well, to cut down on light pollution considering we're in the woods and it's supposed to be serene—not populated by people.

"Do you think you have to throw up?"

She halts on the path. "I don't know." Starts walking again, breathing deep breaths and holding up her hand in the 'stop' motion. "No, I think ish good, ish good."

A few more steps.

Juliet halts again.

I wait, bracing for something I'm not sure is coming, but prepared just the same. Arms out, knees braced, hands at the ready as if I were waiting for an NFL linebacker to come plowing into me, ready for the impact of a fall.

Juliet falters, hands going to her mouth. "Um. I wasn't gonna puke."

Eh. She doesn't look so good, but who am I to say? "I can't take you back inside to puke in the toilet, Juliet, it will back the septic up."

She shakes her pretty head. "Don't know what that means."

"If you're going to toss your cookies, you're going to have to do it in the woods."

"Cookie," she laughs in the way only a drunk person can laugh—a bit maniacal and delirious. "I'm not gonna puke—ish fine. Really, ish fine. You're silly."

I'm silly? Literally never been called that a day in my life, I don't think.

Juliet attempts a few more steps and I wonder how she could have gotten so drunk after only one glass of moonshine; we were all drinking and I don't think any of us got this loaded.

"Juliet, how many glasses of Lionel's booze did you drink?"

"I don't know. Three glasses?"

Three! My eyes almost pop out of their fucking sockets.

Three?

How? *When?* I definitely feel I was paying attention to what she was doing—she's cute and funny and goofy when she's tipsy, but I certainly don't remember her chugging more than one glass of alcohol.

Who poured her another glass?

I was sitting right next to her, surely, I would have noticed?

I'm a big dude and even *I'm* feeling the effects of one glass and the beer I drank to go along with it. It was a chill, relaxing evening—we were all drinking, but Juliet seems to be the only one stumbling her way back to the cottages.

Concerning.

My hand steadies her elbow as I watch her.

Her cheeks puff out and she makes the telltale sign of someone who's going to toss their cookies.

"Oh no," she moans miserably.

Oh *shit*.

"Here, come over here." Gently as I can and as fast as I can, so she doesn't barf in the middle of the walkway where:

1. Anyone can happen upon us and watch.
2. No one will step on it in the dark, or in the morning.

I guide her to the tree line, eyes shifting all over the damn place—for people and for wild animals that may be lurking in the shadows. Last thing I want is to be mauled by a damn bear while I'm performing a civic duty...if there are even bears around.

Juliet is bent over several feet past the path we were taking, hunched over, guts hurling.

"Can you hold my hair?" she moans as she sputters, vomiting into the tall grass. I carefully pull back her smooth ponytail, holding it away from the stream of barf and her mouth, so it stays clean.

Her hair is shiny and silky beneath my fingers and I resist the urge to toy with it. Rub it.

"I'm so ugly!" Juliet cries, literal tears falling from her drunk eyes. "Don't look at me, I'm hideous!"

I laugh at her dismay, thankful she probably won't remember this in the morning.

"I'm so sorry, David."

She's so drunk she can't even get my name right? How is that possible?

I roll my eyes. "It's Davis."

"I can't even get your name right," she moans, spitting

puke onto the pine needled forest floor. "I suck." Juliet pauses. "Actually I don't suck—I haven't given anyone a blow job in ages. I hate being single, but who would even want their dick in this mouth?"

She's crying again, big sloppy tears and loud sobs.

"You're fine. Cute as a button," I lie because in all honesty, this really is not her best look. Not that I've seen all her looks, but a puking Juliet certainly has seen better days. I'm fairly certain she's way cuter when graham cracker vomit isn't spewing from her throat.

Head still bent, hands on her knees, she hurls again.

Gasps. "Ugh. This tastes like chocolate."

I bet it does. She sure ate enough of it. "You're probably throwing up because you ate nine hundred s'mores."

I pat her gently on the back.

"How many?" Her glassy eyes get wide as her head whips up at me.

Shrugging, I'm still holding her ponytail. "Erm, maybe nine hundred?"

"Nine hundred?" she shouts. "Did I? Oh my god, I'm so greedy!"

More sobbing.

"Uh, maybe not that many—I wasn't counting," I lie again. "It was two. Or three." My soothing tone seems to calm her down and her body seems to relax. "I was exaggerating."

"Thank god. Nine hundred is a lot and who—" She pukes into the grass again, wiping her mouth on the sleeve of her sweatshirt.

Ew.

"—who has that many marshmallows even." Carefully she stands, seemingly done doing the deed. "That's like eighty bags at least."

I look away while she sweeps the hair back from her face, pulling some loose strands that have gotten stuck to her lips

"I'm so sorry, David."

Doing my best not to cringe or comment—'cause she's so freaking wasted—my first instinct is to carry Juliet back to the camper and make this job easier. I just don't want to freak her out or scare her, and god forbid, she has to hurl again.

It's slow going getting her back, and eventually, I am able to talk her into bed. I am, however, unable to clean her up— she's practically half asleep by the time we walk to the door and I don't want to wake her up by putting cold water on her face.

Tucking her in, I remove her shoes before slowly creeping out of the room and inching closed the door, making the kitchen table into its convertible sleeping area. I'm definitely way too tall to be comfortable tonight, but it's not like I'm going to climb in the bed with Juliet; can you imagine her waking up in the middle of the night and finding a random dude next to her?

She would probably wake up the entire campground.

Juliet is a determined, stubborn little thing—I know she doesn't care for me and I'm still confused about how she got so damn drunk tonight, vowing to keep a closer eye on her tomorrow for Mia and Thad, though it's not technically my job to do so.

I am not here to babysit, yet here I am babysitting.

Mia and Thad have been lost in their own little world since we arrived—basically MIA. I highly doubt they noticed their little friend downing moonshine and stuffing s'mores into her gullet, let alone be present as she puked her guts out.

I climb onto the makeshift bed, hands clasped behind my head, all the bedding still on the bed in the main sleeping space except for the blanket beneath my ass.

This weekend was supposed to be a bonding trip for the four of us, so we could all get to know each other better, but Mia and Thad have all but abandoned Juliet and I to make lovey-dovey eyes at each other and have sex every opportunity they get.

Don't blame them, but I do miss my buddy time.

I thought we'd be doing more group shit together, not just be getting hooked in the face by errant fish hooks out on the lake followed by a six-hour nap by Juliet.

Hiking?

Checkers?

Canoeing?

Perhaps I'll see if Juliet is up for a boat ride tomorrow—a calm activity may soothe what is sure to be a *massive* hangover; and if I promise to do all the rowing, how will she resist?

I mull this over, contemplating paddles, life jackets and a picnic lunch; wondering how I'm going to get ahold of a few sandwiches, so Juliet and I can steal away tomorrow and leave our best friends in peace.

If I was a betting man, I would wager that Thad and Mia have banged in the woods. Obviously I have no proof of this because obviously I would never ask, but I would be disappointed to find out they haven't done it against a tree.

Lucky bastard.

Bang.

Snap.

The telltale sound of branches breaking outside the camper startles me to an upright position, rattling noises follow that sound like garbage cans being ransacked.

There are zero garbage cans anywhere nearby—the groundskeepers even removed them after the bonfire and I guarantee they lock them up somewhere overnight, so critters don't get them.

Crash.

Bang.

There is definitely something outside.

A shiver goes up my spine.

Could it be a bear?

Jesus, bears scare the shit out of me.

No one needs to know this, but I am a giant chicken shit, afraid of the following:

1. Bears
2. Rabid raccoons
3. Squirrels with a hungry look in their eye
4. Shark infested waters though I've never been in shark infested waters
5. Basically anything that lives in water with teeth, a stinging tail, or spines
6. Large cats of prey
7. Falcons
8. Masked killers from any horror movie

It's an odd list, I know—and doesn't leave much room for the wilderness. Basically, I walk through the woods with one eye on the sky and another over my shoulder, waiting for the next wild animal to make me his next meal, ready to duck for cover.

Snap.

I hear the sound of snapping twigs again, tugging the blanket out from under my ass so I can cover myself with it or at least pull it up to my chin, faster than you can say "HIDE, DAVIS, HIDE!" knowing that there is nothing that can prevent the boogeyman (or whatever is lurking on the other side of this tin foil can I'm stuck inside of) from getting/eating/maiming me if it wants to.

My eyes dart toward the primary guest room as I hunker down, lowering myself, so my head isn't bobbing in front of the window lest the terrors outside spy me and decide to make me a meal.

Oh god, what if it's not an animal? What if it's a mass

murderer? I've seen way too many horror movies, but what if it is?

Chill, Davis, nothing can get you.

"But I'm literally sitting inside a tin can."

Literally.

My brain cannot seem to see reason.

Whatever it is can't get through the door, can it? *Do bears even know how to open doors?* I swear I've seen videos of them waltzing into campers through the front door, but maybe those were circus bears and not bears born in the woods.

Cool it man, it's probably just a raccoon or a hungry squirrel. There is no food nearby, only Juliet's puke.

Right, but the puke is full of chocolate and graham crackers.

Gross. "Could you not go there?"

The fact that I'm talking to myself is not a good sign.

Ben and the rest of the ground staff were busy clearing the campground when we all left for the evening, so no remnants remained—I'm sure of it.

I get out my phone, grateful for the sliver of a satellite signal, googling 'bear gets inside camper,' and 'wild animals in campground,' hunkering down even farther as I watch video after video of black bears in the woods busting through the screen doors of unsuspecting campers and shitting on the furniture, tearing screens, breaking shit.

"Why am I doing this to myself?" I whisper.

I should have left well enough alone.

Because I'm down a rabbit hole! One so deep, I'm not just looking at bear videos, but footage of moose chasing skiers down ski hills, squirrels attacking hikers and collegians on university campuses, cougars and mountain lions on Ring cameras in residential areas.

"A wild animal attack is not how you die, Halbrook." Settle the fuck down, dude. "Take a deep breath."

I take a deep breath.

Five deep breaths.

Count to eleventy.

"Where's a paper bag?" I need a paper bag to breathe in and out of.

Trying to calm my nerves, I get out of my makeshift hovel in an attempt to change from my day clothes and into sweatpants and a hoodie—more comfortable to sleep in if I'm able to drift off with god only knows what lurking beside the camper.

I'm sure it's moved on in search of other things.

Do not look at the window.

"You are six foot three and built like a bull," I pep talk myself.

Not hung like one, but I should be able to defend myself against whatever lurks outside, possibly Juliet too, if worst came to worst.

"I'm huge," I say to absolutely no one. "I could outrun a bear if I had to." Definitely one with a broken leg, or one that had no sight.

Massive paws. Claws.

Teeth.

"Desperation would let me outrun it," I reason, speaking into the dark, turning off all the lights so the bear outside can't see me. "They can climb trees, idiot, you wouldn't be able to get away from one even by dodging and weaving."

Pfft. Whatever.

I'm still super-fast.

"Pow pow—pow!" I punch at the air, my lightning speed prowess no match for the predators outside the camper window. "Light on my feet, light on my feet."

I picture the Davis Halbrook I used to be running down a football field and tearing it up, digging up turf as an ex-running back for a professional football team.

I dodge. Weave.

Score!

A younger Davis Halbrook was naïve.

An athlete wanting to conquer the world before the sport conquered his body and made it impossible for him to perform, taking years and years of physical therapy to get to become the man he is today, so yeah—I could definitely not outrun a damn bear.

My shoulders slouch, defeated at the reality.

"Definitely a bear with a broken leg," I joke to myself, dressed now and staring out into the pitch-black darkness, eyes straining for my glimpse of light or beady eyes shining. "Stop talking to yourself, Halbrook," I whisper. "If Juliet was awake and coherent she would think you were insane."

"Um, I am awake and you do sound insane."

"Oh Jesus!" I whip around, scared shitless, damn near flying off the table that's my bed for the night. The last person I expect to be standing there at this hour of the night, when I'm staring out the window waiting to die at the hands of the unknown, is Juliet. She doesn't sound as drunk as she was a few hours ago when I tucked her in and put her to bed, which surprises me. Maybe it's because she threw up most of the alcohol on the side of the path—maybe it's because she was able to sleep some of it off.

Regardless, I'm embarrassed that she heard me and I hope she won't remember any of this in the morning.

"You gave me a fright."

She's not supposed to be up and out of bed and sounding mostly sober; she's supposed to be passed out so she can't hear the nervous ramblings of a madman in the dark.

Juliet rubs her eyes sleepily with the back of her palms.

"I gave you a *fright*? Did we hop back in time while I was sleeping and go back to the eighteen hundreds?"

"Oh—you went to bed drunk and woke up a comedian?"

I ignore her, climbing up and off my bed. "Are you okay? Do you need anything?"

"I have to pee," she mutters, still sounding drunkish, feeling around the wall for the bathroom door. "Where is the damn light in this god awful place, I can't see where I'm going."

God awful place? Does that mean she hates it in here, too? Or is she just pissed she can't find the toilet?

She grapples, still feeling along. "Where are the lights?"

"Don't turn the light on." I sound like an idiot.

"Why?"

Animals.

Murderers.

Creeps in the other cabins who might be trying to look inside.

Wow, I sound paranoid.

Juliet huffs, irritated, and I imagine her hands on her hips. "Well if I can't turn the light on, how am I supposed to see what I'm doing, *Davis*?"

Pee without the lights, on so the bears don't see us?

Duh. "Haven't you ever had to pee in the dark? How hard can it be for a girl, you don't have to do it standing up and aim for the toilet."

"I have to find the toilet first, you shithead."

So sassy.

"Here, I'll help you." I tap the flashlight on my phone so it shines in her direction, a tiny beacon to guide her.

When Juliet shields her eyes with the crook of her arm, the light flashes in her direction and I notice then that she's not wearing pants anymore.

I avert my eyes even though she can't see me staring. It just seems like the polite thing to do.

The bathroom light flicks on despite my efforts and grumbling and I groan when she accidentally drops the toilet seat, making way too much noise.

Shh, I want to tell her. Quiet, the bears!

I climb back onto my uncomfortable, too small, one blanket "bed".

Inside the bathroom, Juliet coughs, gargles mouthwash at the sink and spits.

There is more cumbersome toilet seat banging, toilet flushing, nose blowing and quite honestly, I wouldn't be surprised at this point if she didn't decide to take a shower.

From my spot on the bed, I hold the flashlight in the direction of the bathroom door when it opens and Juliet's head pops out.

"What are you doing over there?" she groggily asks—I can feel her staring in my direction, the only light my phone. "Are you hiding under blankets?"

She's not supposed to notice that sort of thing; not in her inebriated state.

"No, I'm not hiding under the blankets—I only have one and it's basically a tissue." I hesitate. "Why? Does it look like I'm hiding under blankets?"

"Yes, but I'm the one who's drunk," she jokes, shuffling toward the little bedroom at the back of the camper, feet dragging across the ground. "Okay buddy, I'm going back to bed."

The flashlight ray trails along after her.

Slowly she creeps onto the bed, my small light bouncing shadows throughout the unit. The shape of the faucet in the kitchenette. The bathroom door that's swung back open then crept closed again...

...Juliet's feet as she climbs forward across the mattress on her hands and knees before collapsing in a heap.

I grin.

She's an odd one that little Juliet. I feel like I'm finally beginning to figure her out; at first she was as prickly as a little cactus because she thought she had to be on her friend's behalf. In Juliet's mind, Mia was obviously wearing rose colored glasses when it comes to her boyfriend.

Juliet feels the need to do it for her—the judging and the watching for red flags.

That's a loyal friendship.

I would want my friend to do the same; let me know if he thought the woman I was seeing was in it for the wrong reasons. Money, power, or fame—only one of which I have these days. Once I stopped playing ball, the power and the fame went with it and oddly enough, I wouldn't go back to those days in a million years.

Too many women who didn't love me.

Too many women who only wanted to be photographed with me in public.

Let's not talk about Willa, who I moved into my house, who I found out was using me.

In the next room, Juliet emits a loud snore.

She really relaxed this evening and I don't think it was all due to the alcohol—we've known each other for almost eighteen hours now and she's beginning to thaw toward both Thad and myself—it's clear she doesn't see us as the bad guys anymore.

Well, not *as* bad anyway.

Tonight during the bonfire, she didn't give me "the look" once; didn't shoot a single poison dagger at Thad—intentionally or unintentionally.

I call that a win.

Crack.

Bang.

If whatever is lurking outside would go on its merry way and wander back into the forest, that would be swell.

I cannot sleep knowing something might bust through the flimsy door.

Tossing and turning, it takes hours to fall asleep.

The fact that I don't have a pillow doesn't help matters. The fact that I still smell like a bonfire makes falling asleep even harder.

It's a nearly unbearable night of too little sleep when the sun comes up far too soon for my liking.

In the morning, I wake to the smell of sizzling bacon after dreaming that *I AM bacon. Dancing, frying bacon in a pan. Oh yeah—and in the dream, I have a red bow around my bacon neck while dancing on the frying pan stage, surrounded by lights and butter. Butter? Butter makes no sense, no one fries bacon in butter, how unhealthy does that sound?*

I'm awake now, but also still dreaming. Suddenly I am Pepé Le Pew, the infamous Warner Brothers cartoon skunk, feet rising from the ground to follow the heavenly trail of meats, racing toward it to beat the rush of—

"Davis?" A groggy voice hovers over me as I give the air a long whiff. "What on earth are you doing?"

"Huh?" I crack an eye to see Juliet standing over me, hair falling in waves around her shoulders, wearing a feminine tee shirt with lace and black leggings. It's not an outdoorsy outfit, but it's pretty.

"It looks like you're running in your sleep." She pauses to think. "I had a dog who did that; looked like he was chasing squirrels."

I shield my eyes from the light blaring in all the windows. "I smelled bacon."

"I smell it too." She yawns and stretches, not looking the least bit hungover.

What the fuck?

Anytime I'm hungover, I look like absolute shit.

"Are you sick?" Juliet wants to know, still hovering.

"No?"

She doesn't look convinced, scrunching her nose in my

direction. "You look *so* hungover. Just how drunk were you last night?"

How drunk was *I* last night?

How drunk was *I*?

Her tone makes it sound as if I were the one puking in the tree line last night and not the other way around.

"Pardon me? How drunk was *I*?"

Juliet crosses her arms. "Yeah—how drunk were you? You're in here dreaming about bacon and running in your sleep." Her eyes trail over my body as I lie here. "How did you sleep?"

I slept just fine; I am not the one who passed out rip roaring drunk for a baby bit of moonshine.

"Do you remember *anything* about last night?" I move to a sitting position, back cracking on its own when I stretch, resting my back against the window above the makeshift bed which feels more like a wooden bench.

I'm stiff as a damn board.

"I remember the campfire and eating lots of marsh-mallows."

I narrow my eyes. "And?"

I'm sorry, but I held her hair back as she threw up in the bear laden woods—ergo, I risked my life, so she could barf and not have it clog our septic.

"And..." She shrugs.

"Juliet." I say her name to punctuate the point I'm about to make. "I hate to break it to you, but you ate at least fifteen s'mores last night, had three glasses of moonshine, and capped the evening off by blowing chunks in the woods."

She stands silently blinking at me. "Blowing chunks?"

"Puking? Retch. Spew. Yak. Refunded your snacks. Round trip meal ticket. Vomcano—"

"I get it, I get it." Juliet blinks again as if mentally piecing the evening together and coming up short. She scoffs indignantly and from my vantage point, I can see straight up her nose. "I think I would remember if I threw up."

Her fingers touch her lips.

"You and I both know you woke up fully clothed—the same way I did—because you were sauced, but also: can we talk about how impressed I am with myself right now for coming up with all those acronyms for barf?" I feel like a bloody genius actually.

The smug expression is wiped off my cellmate's—I mean, roommate's—face. "I did not actually throw up." Her hand is still at her mouth. "Did I?"

"You did. Which is probably what attracted the bears last night." Yes, they could have been raccoons, but it's more dramatic to go with bears, and I'm feeling woodsy and festive, so *bears it is.*

Juliet's eyes are huge. "Bears?"

"Yes, something was outside last night circling the camper."

I think.

I mean—it's just a guess and it could have been a skunk, but still. Something was outside.

"What was it?"

I shake my head solemnly. "Don't know. All I know is that it wanted in." I pause for dramatic effect and throw off my one, thin cover. "It wanted in really bad."

Her face is pale. "How do you know?"

"I could hear it rattling things. Breaking branches." Three. Two. One. "*Breathing.*"

"You could hear it breathing?"

I nod. "I stayed up all night listening, just in case."

"Just in case what?"

"In case I had to defend us."

She eventually stops beleaguering the discussion and moves to give me space; the incredulous expression never leaving her face. I rise from the stiff and rickety makeshift bed —I know it's an actual bed that actual people sleep on, but it's definitely not made for men my size.

I can literally hear my body cracking when I move and Juliet hears it, too, if the cringe on her face is any indication.

I feel her watching me as I move about the cabin, ransacking my duffle to find fresh clothes; I hadn't packed a ton and planned on re-wearing stuff, but hadn't planned on nightly bonfires that left me smelling like a wood burning pit and probably a little barf, too.

None got on me, but it also might have.

"Random question," Juliet's timid voice follows me as I make for the tiny bathroom. "Um, by any chance, did anyone oversee my, um, incident?"

"Incident?"

Her hands wave dramatically about the air.

"You know, the *incident*." She lowers her voice. "Me throwing up outside."

Ah.

I grin. "That wasn't throwing up. That was drunk puking."

"Can we not call it that?"

"You don't want to call it throwing up or puking?"

"I'd rather not."

Women are so weird sometimes.

"But that's what you were doing," I argue. "Why do you want to pretty it up with different words?"

"Yes please." She laughs and I think it's the first time I've heard it ,so my head snaps around and I stare, trying to get a glimpse of her naturally smiling face and watching her from the doorway.

Wow.

Just...wow. Juliet is really something when she's smiling and I try not to gawk, but damn.

Color me surprised; she is so damn adorable.

Granted, I've seen her smile plenty in the past twenty-four hours, but there seems to be a huge difference in her fake smiling to be polite and this natural grinning at me while she's joking.

Her teeth aren't perfectly straight and white, and her lips aren't as full as most women want their lips these days, but everything about her face is perfect anyway.

Wait.

That was sort of a backhanded compliment, wasn't it?

Yikes.

Thank God I didn't say any of that out loud; she'd probably smack me in the balls.

"No one saw you ralphing in the bushes, I promise you. Maybe a deer or two or a possum, but no actual human beings."

At least not that I'm aware of—for all I know Steve and Paul could've been watching out their camper window, or Erik and Cookie could've been canvassing the forest for fuck buddies.

Not likely, but possible.

Juliet's face falls. "I'm so embarrassed." Her cheeks puff out a breath of air. "I can't remember the last time I got drunk and I'm so sorry you had to see me like that."

"You apologized last night..." My voice is gloating. "...as I was holding back your hair, so you didn't puke on it."

Her embarrassed face turns to one of anger. "You're the worst!"

"I'm the *best* for holding your hair back and putting you to bed."

I laugh, ducking as she tosses a sweatshirt in my direction. Luckily it's flimsy and never makes it the entire way, falling instead on the fake hardwood floor in the camper.

"How am I the worst because I'm telling the truth? Enlighten me."

"No one wants to be reminded that they did something stupid."

"Especially you?"

"I do my best not to make an ass of myself in public if I can help it." She blushes, ducking to hide her face.

"Don't worry—you didn't make an ass of yourself in front of anyone—you just couldn't hold your liquor and honestly, I had a hard time not throwing up myself. That shit was strong." I have no idea what Lionel put in that moonshine, but it most likely contains gasoline and gunpowder.

Woo wee, it was some strong shit.

"You're just saying that to make me feel better," she pouts, bending to pick up the sweatshirt she'd just thrown. Juliet folds it in her arms, hugging it to her body as if it were a blanket.

"Trust me, I wouldn't just say that to make you feel better. It was a little odd that you kept eating s'mores, but other than that, everyone else was drunk too and didn't notice—that I'm aware of." Mostly.

Buzzed at the very least?

"Really? Are you just saying that to make me feel better?"

One hundred percent.

"Each and every last one of them was sauced."

"For real?"

I hold up a hand and cross my fingers. "Scout's Honor."

Juliet sighs. "You're probably lying about being a Boy Scout, too."

"I never said I was a Boy Scout—all I said was Scout's Honor," I laugh. "I didn't have time for clubs, I was too obsessed with football."

My mother worked full-time and my dad was never in the picture—Mom didn't have time or the resources to be driving me and my younger sister from one activity to the next, so I chose football. Damn she was relieved when I got a full-ride scholarship to college; more relieved when I not only got drafted, but I'd earned a degree, too.

Plan B, she said.

And Mom wasn't wrong—I sure as hell needed that fallback the minute my knee gave out during a playoff game, ending my professional career.

Juliet takes advantage of my silent reflection, giving me a once-over. She starts at my feet, gaze traveling up my legs, waist and chest, neutral expression never faltering.

I can't for the life of me tell what she's thinking, but I hope it's '*Wow, Davis is so incredibly handsome and good-looking. Loves animals, is wonderful with children. Bet he would make someone the perfect boyfriend, maybe I should hook him up with one of my friends.*'

Sighing, I ease my big body into the minuscule bathroom and slide closed the door.

CHAPTER 5

Juliet

W *hat on earth is Davis Halbrook doing behind that tree?* I have the thought as I make my way down the trail to the pier with a book clutched in one hand, bottle of water in the other, my suspicions of him causing my eyes to narrow in his direction.

All I can see is the back of his head, back, and ass popping out, the tall oak tree concealing whatever it is he's doing.

Hmm.

Weird.

In general, I don't necessarily think that Davis is weird. Over the past twenty-four hours he's actually proven to be a relatively decent guy, if putting me to bed after a night of drinking is any indication of his moral fiber. He hasn't tried anything with me and he hasn't been a jerk.

Quite the opposite in fact, Davis is personable, funny and seems to be winning over everyone at the campground. I eyeball him as I meander down the path, the romance novel in my hand taking second fiddle.

For real, what is he doing?

Needing to investigate, I change direction and make my

way toward him. I'm not loud, so it doesn't appear that he hears me as he continues to stand in the same position. Instead of approaching him from behind, I approach him from the front, making an arch, so that I'm not sneaking up on him.

God knows I don't want to scare the crap out of the guy by approaching from the back, although the idea does make me smile.

He seems to scare easily, the way he rambled on and on about bears last night.

I might have been drunk, but I don't suffer from drunk amnesia, remembering quite well his panicked word vomit as he tried to act tough.

Stepping off the pea gravel walkway, I move around the tree and see water spraying out the front side of the tree, my eyes and my brain not making the connection at the same time, the delay far too late when I'm standing directly in front of my roommate.

"Oh my god, you're peeing!"

"Jesus!" he shouts in reply, hand holding his dick as he stands peeing on the ground.

"Oh my god, shit!"

"Shit!"

Don't look, don't look, don't look, I tell myself, willing myself not to look down and follow the stream of urine up to his penis and *God, why am I still standing here?*

This is a private moment.

On the other hand, he's in public.

Er, sort of.

"Why aren't you in the bathroom?" I ask, slightly affronted by the entire situation.

"What do you mean why aren't I in the bathroom, we're in the woods!"

"So? Obviously anyone could come along and see you!"

"We're in the woods!" he says again. "And I have a dick, I don't need to pee inside!"

"Why are you yelling?" I ask, crossing my arms and lowering my tone because he's right, and I'm just embarrassed and projecting onto him.

Davis goes about shaking the remaining pee from his cock and stuffing everything back into his jeans, zipping them up and placing his hands on his hips.

"Don't even start that nonsense."

Nonsense?

I laugh, holding the book up to my face, shielding my grinning mouth.

"Oh now you think this is funny?"

I lower my head. "I didn't get a look at anything, honest."

Sadly.

I mean—not that dicks are pretty or fun to look at, but I'd be lying if I said I wasn't curious. What girl wouldn't be?

Big, small, shower, grower: inquiring minds want to know!

Over the top of my book, my gaze goes lower to the front of his jeans—not on purpose, but because they have a mind of their own and right now, that mind seems to be in the gutter.

Listen, it's been a long time since I've been laid and I'm warm blooded, no matter what thoughts I had when I came into this vacation that isn't my idea of a fun vacation.

More like summer camp on steroids with less fun, no counselors, and more alcohol.

"Stop trying to check out my package, you had your chance when you snuck up on me."

He begins walking back toward the trail.

"I wasn't sneaking up on you. I didn't realize you were peeing until I almost walked into it."

"What the hell did you think I was doing behind the tree? Playing a game?"

"No." My head is shaking as I follow behind him, trying to keep up. "I wasn't thinking at all."

He glances at me over his shoulder and raises his heavy brows. "I thought you didn't like me, why are you following me?"

"I'm not—just so happens, I'm headed in this direction. Don't flatter yourself."

"I never flatter myself." He snorts.

"Oh please—you know you're good-looking." The words come flying out of my mouth before I can stop them and I immediately press them shut, so more dumb things don't come out.

Davis stops walking and spins around. "You think I'm good-looking?"

Now I'm the one snorting. "I didn't say that." Well, not in those words.

"No, you said, '*Oh please—you know you're good-looking,*' which means you think I'm good-looking." He raises his voice a few octaves, which I'm assuming is his best Juliet impression.

I am not impressed.

My chin tilts up as I roll my eyes up to the treetops. "You're taking it out of context."

"Right. We were talking about you following me and stalking me and not looking at me, and then you said I was good-looking as if that were a defense."

I want to wipe that cocky grin off his face, but he's not wrong; the problem is, I can't talk my way out of this corner I put myself in, dammit.

"It's too early for this conversation." Dramatically I press a hand to my forehead and furrow my brow, feigning a cringe. "I have a hangover."

Davis laughs. "You are not hungover. You said so this morning."

Did I?

"I don't recall." Plenty of greasy bacon, buttery toast, and chocolate milk for breakfast definitely did the trick, curing me of whatever post-alcohol induced ailments I may have had.

I stomp down the path, staring at his broad back, affronted that he's calling me out on my bullshit.

Rude.

I don't want to like him. I don't want to like Thad.

But they're both so LIKEABLE AND ANNOYING.

Ugh.

"Where you headed?" he wants to know, making small talk. "Thad took Mia to town for lunch."

They left? They left and didn't say good-bye? Or offer to bring me an actual coffee from an actual coffee shop?

It's been two whole days since I've had a latte.

Okay, that's a strike in the negative column against both Thad AND my best friend—this whole trip was supposed to be a bonding experience for the four of us, but it's turning into a romantic getaway for Thad and Mia, and they've ditched us most of the time we've been here!

What the actual hell, man!

We're in the woods! I don't want to fend for myself!

I don't want to come up with my own activities!

I need to be shown where the fun is! I'm not built for trees, sticks, water and bald eagles flying overhead. Campers with tiny showers and tiny sinks and beds that convert into tables and tables that convert into beds with barely any room for luggage.

"When will they be back?"

Davis shrugs. "Don't know, he didn't say. I didn't even realize they were leaving and caught them as they were climbing into the Gator to be taken to the outpost for their ride."

"I hate this place," I grumble, kicking at a rock. "What are we supposed to do all day, stare at each other?"

Davis stops again, except this time, I'm clomping along so intently, I almost smash into him.

"We?"

I roll my eyes. "Who else am I supposed to hang out with? Lionel who tried to kill me with his moonshine or Cookie who wants to sleep with you?"

He ignores most of my sentence. "Are you implying that you want to spend the day with me?"

"No, I'm implying that I don't want to sit around twiddling my thumbs and be bored." Although I do have this book, one I haven't started, but that got great reviews. "I could find a hammock and read or something, at least until lunch." I sneak a peek up at his face. "Unless you have a better idea."

He seems to mull this over, raising his hand to touch his ear where I'd hooked him. "Fishing is out of the question—all of the boats have been reserved, and I have no intention of having my eyes gouged out with hooks or you accidentally hitting me in the back of the head with the pole." He runs that same hand across the stubble on his chin. "And it's too cold right now to go swimming."

Swimming? In the lake? Hard pass.

Davis goes on as we stand in the middle of the path. The resort feels empty, not a single person in sight except the man rearranging the campfire pit, another one neatly setting water bottles out on a table nearby in tidy rows.

"So what are our options?"

A hmm sound comes from his throat. "I don't know, maybe we should Google it."

Google it? Is he being serious?

I pull my phone out of my back pocket and Google 'things to do at campgrounds'.

"What does it say?" He's leaning over now, invading my personal space, smelling woodsy and fresh and really, really good smelling.

"Um..... Read books and magazines." I hold up my book to show him that was on my list of things to do.

"A romance novel? I wouldn't have taken you for a romance novel girl."

"What the heck is that supposed to mean?"

"I mean—you seem more like a crime and murder kind of person."

I have no idea if that's meant to be a compliment or not, but I'm going with *not*.

"Gee, thanks."

Davis isn't picking up on my sarcasm, and nods. "What else can we do?"

"Besides ask Ben?" I consult the list on my phone. "Read out loud to each other."

Davis laughs, snatching the book from my hand and flipping it over, so he can peruse the description on the back, reading it out loud. *"I would do anything for my best friend. Well.* Almost *anything. When she begs me to come on a weekend getaway, so I can bond with her new boyfriend, I can't say no—no matter how badly I want to. After all, who will keep an eye on the guy; he's your stereotypical, professional football player—emphasis on* player—*and I* don't *trust him with my friend's heart."*

He bursts into pealing laughter, tears actually forming in his eyes. "What is this crap? It's killing me."

I snatch the book back from him, glaring.

"Can you imagine reading that out loud to me?"

"No—you're very rude." Nonetheless, my eyes go back to the list. "Crafting, knitting, sewing." I roll my eyes. "Board games? Puzzles." Okay, that might not be the worst idea—I could do a board game. I kick ass at Scrabble and Monopoly...

"Does that seriously say 'Make up stories to tell each other'?"

"I assume they mean around the campfire."

"This is the worst fucking list, with the worst fucking ideas, I've ever seen in my life. Who wrote this, a ten-year-old at sleep-away camp?"

I wish he would stop reading over my shoulder and breathing into my ear.

"What kind of ideas were you going for, Sparky? Cliff diving, cave exploring?"

"Uh—yeah, those are exactly the kind of ideas I was looking for, smart ass. Who wants to sit around and crochet when they could be diving off a cliff?"

"Well you just said it was too cold to swim, so...yeah." I would literally shit my pants if I had to jump from a cliff into a watery grave, so bless his heart for being a wuss.

"Does that say skipping stones? I did that already."

That causes me to look up at him. "You did? When?"

"When we first got here, I was bored."

Huh. Interesting.

"Disc golf, lawn bowling, horseshoes, tennis, badminton." He glances around. "Why do they have none of those things."

"We're supposed to be roughing it."

"Um, I'm sorry, but that tent Thad is staying in cannot, by any stretch, be considered roughing it."

"I meant us. They're doing this to torture us."

Davis nods. "Sounds accurate. I've barely seen either of them and it's getting on my last nerve."

"Well we only have one night left, and then we can go back to the real world where there are snacks, Wi-Fi and activities."

His nose is in my hair as he asks, "What the fuck is spelunking?"

We search for that definition, too. "Spelunking, known as caving, is an increasingly popular sport—you walk, climb or crawl blindly into the darkness with only a headlamp, spiders, and bats for company. The difficulty level and danger, not unlike hiking or rock climbing, varies widely."

"Dude, that sounds awesome."

"Really Davis? Does it?" Because to me it sounds like hell on earth and if that's something he wants to do today, he can do it by his own self, *thankyouverymuch*.

"Relax, Juliet, I wasn't suggesting we do it today, I just said it sounded awesome." He ruffles my hair. "Oh look—the list says we can catalog rocks."

"No."

"Bug collecting?"

"Immediately no."

"Nature gathering, searching for wild berries, nuts and other edible plants."

"This is the nerdiest list I've ever seen in my entire life," I muse. "Although we could play hide-and-seek. You hide, I'll seek you...in about five hours."

"Har har." He chuckles. "You'd kill me with wild berries, for sure."

"Oh absolutely!" I grin, enjoying the banter. "Swing in a hammock, watch the breeze blowing the trees that sounds like it would be fun for about thirty seconds."

"You have no patience."

"Fine—you go swing in the breeze and watch trees blow."

"Daydream and let your mind wander," he reads aloud.

"I already do that, like—every single day." In fact, if I got paid to let my mind wander, I'd be rich and living in London, having high tea every day and eating bon-bons.

"Try out new varieties of s'mores."

My stomach churns at the thought. "Ugh, I'm not touching one of those again for a very long time."

"Same, not after watching you toss them up on the walk home."

If he could stop reminding me that would be fantastic.

He sighs in my ear. "We can't stand here all day discussing this, we need to settle on something."

"But all these ideas are stupid," I say petulantly, not having ideas of my own to contribute.

"We could take a walk, go hiking or something."

"Yeah—we could." Not that I *want* to, but it is something to do.

"We can have a countdown to lunch, then race back," Davis suggests helpfully.

I give him a side-eye. "Racing through the woods sounds like a great way to get your eye poked out with a stick."

"Please—it's safer than being in a fishing boat with you and your hooks."

True story.

We shuffle along the path, going nowhere because we have no plan of action, laughing and talking the entire way. It's a nice companionable chat that I find myself easing into as if it were natural and we've known one another longer than twenty-four hours.

Strange considering what an entitled ass I was, demanding he get his own space when there are no other spaces for him to sleep in. Not to mention, he slept on the kitchen table last night, fully clothed, with only a thin blanket.

Guilt rears its ugly head at me.

What a spoiled brat I'm being.

We spend the next few hours as I originally planned; reading in a hammock down near the shore, me swinging in one with the paperback book open to Chapter One and Davis swinging in another with a ball cap pulled down over his eyes.

He doesn't ask me to read to him out loud, which oddly disappoints me. I think it would be funny to watch his facial expressions as I read him a romance novel, especially the spicy parts or when they get romantic and have sex. Although now that I think about it that would probably be too embarrassing, reading the specifics out loud to the nearest stranger. I could see myself reading out loud to someone I was dating though; it might be fun foreplay.

At one point he raises the cap and looks over at me; asks if I'm hungry.

"Did you get the memo? I'm always hungry." I squint as the sun shines through the trees. "What time is it?"

"It's only eleven o'clock," he says. "But they should be putting food out pretty soon for lunch."

"Not that you're keeping track," I laugh.

"Not that I'm keeping track, but I am also always hungry. Could always eat. Basically I'm like my little niece—she's always at my house and digging in my fridge because she knows I have good stuff. My sister is always feeding her healthy food."

That was a mouthful.

"Your niece?"

"Yeah. They live right next-door."

"They? You mean your sister and her family live right next-door?"

"No, it's just my sister and her daughter. There's no husband in the picture. I kind of take care of them in a way, but I don't?"

I wonder what that means, and pry for more details. Try as I may, I cannot resist the urge to be nosy. "What do you mean?"

He shrugs, lowering the hat again and covering his eyes. "My dad was never in the picture and we were raised by a single mom. So when Penelope got pregnant with Skipper and it became obvious her father wasn't going to be in the picture, I bought her the house next door."

Oh.

Oh. My. God.

My heart squeezes and grows two sizes.

DAMMIT.

No, Juliet—no! You will not succumb to his generosity.

Okay, but he also volunteers at the Humane Society.

Big deal, tons of people love animals, that does not make him special.

Not make him special? Now you're just being an asshole.

I shake my head to clear the feathers out of it. "How old is your niece?"

"Seven."

Seven?

My heart pitter patters with an undeniable 'awwww.' Seven. What a fun, cute, age.

"My sister works full-time, so she's over a lot." His mouth is moving and because his eyes are covered, I can study his full lips without him noticing, the five o'clock shadow from his lack of shaving only highlighting the cleft in his chin and the smile lines beside his mouth.

Ugh, I love that.

No you don't. You are a weak, weak woman who hasn't had a date in months.

Stop talking to yourself!

Reluctantly I let the subject drop and go back to my book; I'm insatiably curious but don't want to come off as being intrusive. He's already given me more details about himself than he's given me the past twenty-four hours we've been together—granted, I was either sleeping or drunk for a lot of our time and wouldn't remember even if he had told me.

It's a very personal detail for him to reveal that he bought his sister a home and that he takes care of his niece to help her out. It also says a lot about him, his valuing family, and making it a priority to take care of his sibling. Briefly I wonder if she is his only sister, but push the thought away, as I start chapter two of my book, other questions lingering in my mind.

How often do you watch your niece?

What kind of uncle are you?

When is the last time you had a girlfriend?

Were you ever engaged?

Random things that are none of my business, I do my best to focus on the words in front of me even as Davis's cologne drifts my way with every, blissful breeze.

My eyes scan the pages of my book, reading them over and over again, not retaining a single word.

Sighing, I give the air one more sniff, not able to stop myself.

CHAPTER 6
Davis

"Dude, you could have told us you were leaving today. We're sort of butthurt y'all aren't spending time with us."

Thad is cracking open a bottle of beer and leaning against the porch of my shared camper.

"Sorry, Mia wanted some alone time."

I glance around at the solitude. "Um, we're in the middle of nowhere. How much more alone time could you possibly have? You dragged us here to bond with you."

"I know, but with traveling and being on the road for work, she and I don't actually spend much time together. This seemed like a good idea at the time, but now that it's actually happening...the woods might have been a stretch."

"You think? Juliet and I had jack shit to do today while you love birds were off having lunch prepared by actual chefs."

"Oh come on—it couldn't have been that bad. Juliet was prickly at the beginning, but you have to admit, she's coming around."

Yeah, I don't think she hates him as much as she tried to in the beginning, which is indeed good news. For him.

"So what did the two of you do while we were gone? Take one of the boats out and do some more fishing? I think Ben said something about the pontoon boat being available." Thad has an orange in his hand and begins gnawing on one of the slices.

Pontoon boat ride? That might have been fun.

"No, we ended up lounging around most of the day in the hammocks. Juliet read a book and I took a nap, and then we had lunch. Super chill and low-key, you didn't miss anything."

"Any sparks?"

Sparks?

My best friend has the audacity to ask about *sparks*? The idea of me dating anyone new has never entered our conversation; Thad knows that I'm still taking time for myself after my last breakup.

"No there weren't any sparks, what are you talking about? The woman practically hates me."

"No one hates you," he says with a laugh. "Absolutely no one. Literally everyone loves you, including small animals and old people."

He's not wrong, but a lot of it has to do with the fact that I volunteer a lot. It's not hard to win people over when you give a shit about them. Give a crap about the plight of humanity and try to make the world a better place—it tends to soften people who would ordinarily not take a shine to you. People like Juliet, with her preconceived notions of my best friend and I. No matter how much she tries to deny it, I know that she was judging us because we are professional athletes; or at least, one of us is.

"Aww, buddy." I put my hand on Thad's shoulder and squeeze. "Are you saying you love me?"

"Yeah, man, I love you. You're my best friend."

"In the whole wide world?"

He shrugs my hand off his shoulder with a laugh. "Not in

the whole wide world, bro, only my mom can claim that title. If I wasn't her best friend, she'd kill me."

"Dude—only you would be best friends with your mom."

He and his mom are close; in fact, both his parents are so far up his ass I'm shocked he's able to have a fully functioning romantic relationship. Carol is great, but judgmental: no one is good enough for her baby boy. The boy she raised into a man, raised into a superstar.

Mia is a saint for putting up with his mother's antics.

I'm shocked Carol hasn't moved into Thad's guest room at this point; she hired and manages his housekeeper, organizes his nutrition and keeps his fridge stocked—all via zoom because they summer in the Midwest and winter in Florida and Thad is on the East Coast most of the year.

"Look, sometimes the only people you can trust are your parents."

He's not wrong, but—at some point you have to trust your partner.

It didn't work in my favor obviously or I'd still be in a relationship with...dammit. I don't even want to say her name or use it in a sentence or think it, for that matter.

I thought my ex-girlfriend was a decent person. I thought she loved me, I thought she loved my sister, niece and my mom. Turns out, it was just an act because she wanted to marry some rich guy—or a guy she perceived as rich—and settle into a lifestyle where she would never have to work again.

Listen, I'm all for a partner who wants to stay home. Work from home or stay home and raise kids. What I have a problem with is someone who lies about their intentions from the start, pretending to be someone they are not with an end goal of being pampered and given gifts and a lifetime of Botox and fillers in their face to keep them looking gorgeous without having to work for any of it.

And by work, I mean: put effort into the relationship. Getting to know me. Getting physical with me. Showing affection.

Once she thought she was getting what she wanted, all that stopped. Once she moved into my house, she changed.

Began ordering my housekeeper around, gave my sister hours that she and Skipper could swing by, wouldn't let me touch her on certain nights of the week.

It was embarrassing and insulting.

You may be wondering why I fell for a girl like that to begin with and the truth is, I still don't know myself. I thought about it endlessly. My sister had known it all along, of course, and had warned me. But there's only so much listening a man who thinks he's in love will do, you know? I thought I knew Willa. I thought she was a good person. Hell, I even thought she loved volunteering the same way I do, but it turns out that was a lie just like everything else. What Willa loved was designer purses and free rent.

Our first Christmas together, after only dating six months, she made me a list and presented it so I could do my Christmas shopping, get her some things that she wanted—and nothing she didn't. God forbid I get her a simple sweater or plain hoop earrings.

There was nothing on that list under one thousand dollars.

I remember my jaw hitting the floor when I held the paper and yet, the red flag still hadn't started waving until I came home one afternoon and overheard her in the kitchen with Skipper. She was telling my niece, who was six years old at the time, that she would no longer be allowed to come and go as she pleased—she would have to text her first.

Her. *Willa.*

Text Willa, not Uncle Davis.

Total bullshit.

The whole thing was devastating to me; as devastating as it was to Skipper and my sister, having some woman basically kick them out after I'd supported them for years. "The gravy train is over," Willa had told my niece. She didn't realize that she wasn't the gravy train—I was and she was on the receiving end of it, too. Only Willa was too selfish and stubborn to admit it, acting as if she was the one occasionally doling out the money for bills and groceries to my sister and not me.

Besides, it wasn't actually any of her business what I did with my money at that point; we weren't married, engaged, or anything of the sort.

"The point is," Thad is rambling on, half of his babble I missed from woolgathering. "Everyone loves you and I don't get why Juliet doesn't have her nose up your ass like everyone else does."

"No one has their nose up my ass."

"Sure they do." He pops another piece of orange in his mouth and chews. "That woman at your gym."

"Sheila? She's the manager. She has to be friendly."

His shrug is noncommittal. "Okay, what about that woman at the place where you buy your pants?"

I roll my eyes. "All these women are in retail. They have to like me so they can make money off of me."

He relents. "True, but admit it, you're a neat guy."

Neat.

Never been described as neat before, but hey—I'll take it. "Thanks, bro, you're neat too."

"I would date you."

"Thanks, man. I feel the same way about you."

Juliet comes walking up the path just then, stopping to watch Thad and I embrace, a slow shake of her head as a smile crosses her lips.

Thad and I pull apart, doing the back pat as we move away.

"No, no—please, don't let me interrupt your bromance."

"We were done being mushy with each other—you weren't interrupting anything," Thad says. "Besides, every day is a bromance with this guy around."

Juliet's eyes shift to me. "I bet."

Thad nudges me in the ribcage and I nudge him back. The last thing I need is him playing matchmaker with a woman who doesn't seem to have any interest in me. If she had her way, I'd be sleeping on the cold, hard ground beneath the camper—not inside of it.

Besides. I haven't heard her mention jack shit about herself since we've been cooped up together.

I literally know nothing about her; as far as I know, we have zero things in common. It's possible she doesn't like animals or small children, or even want children of her own.

I want a family. Apparently finding a woman willing to bear one is more difficult than I'd thought it would be.

Still, Juliet hasn't been a complete shrew like I'd feared would be the case the morning we met. Damn she was prickly that morning.

Then again—we were all standing over her as she slept; I wouldn't want to wake up surrounded by my friends gawking over my lifeless body, either, as if I were in a casket.

So weird.

I make a mental note to ask her some questions tonight; I'm sure we'll be next to each other again at tonight's bonfire —tonight is the last hurrah on our quick getaway before we head out tomorrow.

In the past thirty-six something hours I've managed to:

1. Barely get any sleep
2. Worried about bear attacks
3. Walked too fast through the woods after dark to avoid said bears

4. Hardly gotten any exercise or exerted myself unless it was after dark
5. Worried about my sister and niece, as per usual
6. Worried about bear attacks

I cannot live on picnic food and pudgy pies alone, so thank goodness we're heading home tomorrow. I leave at first light, one of the first to set off since my flight is in the morning. Not ideal but I have things to do and people to see and hate waiting around at the airport.

Ben wasn't thrilled when he learned I would need my own ride; none of the other campers/guests require a shuttle that early in the day, so they have a bus coming for the entire group.

Back in the camper, I prepare for tomorrow morning by throwing most of my things in the duffle bag so I don't have to do it when I wake up; it'll probably still be dark out and Lord knows I won't want to turn on any of the lights in the camper to avoid waking up Juliet. I've seen her in the morning and the last thing I want to do is wake the proverbial bear—not that she's a monster in the morning, but there's no sense in making any more commotion than necessary.

After I get everything sorted—there isn't a whole lot considering I under packed—I make my way back down the path where everyone has gathered around, yet another campfire. It seems that this whole weekend consisted of nothing but, if you don't count the one day we attempted to go fishing.

I reach for my ear and squeeze the lobe where I'd been hooked, the memory making me smile. The look on Juliet's face when she'd realized her line was attached to my head was actually pretty priceless. The horrified expression will be burned into my brain forever and most likely hers, too.

Hilarious.

Not at the time, but...yeah.

Hilarious.

Juliet doesn't show herself until we're all seated around the campfire, though this time she makes it in time for dinner. They're serving barbeque and chicken kabobs, pasta salads and brownies for dessert—all things I could eat and eat and eat and eat.

"You really love that outfit, don't you?" I ask when she plops down beside me yielding a paper plate loaded down with food, wearing the same sweatshirt and jeans she's had on the two previous days.

"This is the only thing I have that's appropriate to wear."

What on earth does that mean? "Do you have a suitcase full of scandalous clothing?"

Juliet picks the chicken kabob off her plate and nibbles on the grilled mushroom capping off the end. "No, Davis—it means I have a suitcase full of cute sundresses and bikinis."

I haven't made a plate for myself as my stomach is well aware, protesting with a loud grumble. Instead of standing and moving to the buffet, I give Juliet another once-over.

"Why would you bring sundresses and bikinis on a wilderness vacation?"

She halts chewing long enough to freeze me with a stare hard enough to emasculate most men. "Because Davis, I thought we were going somewhere warm and sunny and tropical." She sighs, setting the chicken down in the center of her plate, licking her fingers. "Like the Caribbean."

Um. "Why?"

She seems embarrassed, fidgeting in her collapsible chair. "I don't know. I guess I assumed we were going on a beach vacation?"

"Ah. That makes sense." Yeah, no to the beach vacation. "It's not really Thad's style and Mia had seen this place on the internet and fell in love."

Juliet rolls her eyes heavenward. "Ha ha. She's super outdoorsy."

"Wait., is that sarcasm?"

"Oh, you're picking up on that?" More sarcasm.

"Are you implying Mia *isn't* outdoorsy?"

I glance over at Thad and his girlfriend, with her jet-black hair shining in the firelight, makeup done to perfection though we're hardly in the environment for glam.

Is Mia not who she says she is? Could she be pretending?

She has never come off as a gold digger to me, but I'm probably not the best person to be judging; I've been fooled by way too many women.

I have zero spidey senses when it comes to people taking advantage of me.

I study Mia while Juliet picks at her food with her fingers rather than her fork.

"Um.... I would never throw my best friend under the bus like that."

"But you're also not denying it."

"Listen, she wouldn't be the first woman in the world to lie about her interests to get a man's attention."

I don't love the sound of that.

When I have no reply, Juliet turns to face me, catching a good glimpse of my face.

"Shit—that is not what I meant. She's not...Mia isn't..." Juliet sets her plate on her lap and scoots her chair over, leaning over and lowering her voice. "Listen to me. She is not like that—I can see what you're thinking by the look on your face and it's not like that at all. Trust me."

"Trust you? I know nothing about you and we've been sharing a toilet for two days."

She nods slowly. "You have a good point. Alright—ask me anything you want and I'll answer it."

I narrow my eyes but my mouth is smiling. "Is this a trick?"

Juliet laughs. "No. I'm admitting you are right; you don't know me. I mean—we don't have to be best friends but I want you to trust my best friend, so if I have to pony up a little information to do that—so be it." She hesitates, taking her plate up again and forking some pasta salad. "I love a good Q and A."

Same.

I follow a few Would You Rather pages on Instagram like the giant nerd I am and love asking the questions to Skipper as much as she loves answering them.

"Fine, you have a deal, but first let me grab something to eat because I'm freaking starving."

Juliet nods and resumes eating while I rise and get some food of my own, heaping baked beans onto the plate that I'll definitely regret later, a bun filled with pulled pork BBQ, tater tots (which feel like a random addition to the lineup but still welcome), pasta salad, corn on the cob, and not one, but *two* brownies.

I sit back down.

We eat in silence while everyone else around us chats, and I scan my eyes over at Thad and Mia; she has her hand on his forearm and is caressing it, coy smile on her face that seems to say *'let's get out of there and bang in the woods while no one is paying attention to us'*.

I shove the sandwich in my mouth and feel the sauce dripping down my chin, remembering too late I didn't grab a napkin.

Juliet comes to my rescue. "Here. Looks like you need a bib."

"Thanks," I mumble with a mouthful. "This is so good—I was starving."

She nods.

She also seems to be watching me warily, wondering what my first question will be perhaps?

"Where do you live?" I blurt out.

"Are you asking for my address?" She quirks her brow.

"No. I mean what city are you in?" For all I know she's clear across the United States.

"I live about fifteen minutes from Mia in Libertyville."

Oh shit.

"Why?" Juliet wants to know.

She's not far from me.

I shrug. "For a second there I wasn't sure if you lived in Illinois at all."

"Ahh. Makes sense."

"Do you have any pets?"

"No, but not because I don't love animals—it's because I live in an apartment and I don't think it would be fair for an animal to be cooped up." Juliet pauses. "I'm more of a dog person, so..."

Same.

Juliet munches on her pasta. "What about you? Do you have any pets?"

"I used to have two dogs when I played football but I'd always need a friend to watch them anytime I traveled. My buddy Pete has this huge, fenced in yard where they could run and run—then he and his wife had a few kids, and the dogs freaking loved them and the kids loved the dogs," I muse as I continue eating my sandwich. "Eventually I felt like an asshole taking them home with me so...now they live with Pete and Shannon."

"That seems like the humane thing to do," Juliet tells me approvingly. "I would absolutely love to have a dog, I just don't have room for the kind of dog that I want. You know, the big retriever type that needs a ton of exercise? I don't think I could do that without a partner—I know myself well enough to know that I'm not going to walk a dog like that every day or even take it to a dog park."

She hesitates before adding, "God that makes me sound like such a jerk."

"That doesn't make you an asshole or a jerk," I tell her. "That makes you self-aware. Do you know how many people get animals that they shouldn't have, and then the animal suffers?" I dig my fork into the pasta salad on my plate. "Drives me nuts and it ends up filling the shelters with dogs that were placed in the wrong homes to begin with."

There are times of doubt about getting another dog, but I do some traveling, and I would hate to lean on Penelope when I'm gone. It's not her job to take care of my things, especially *living* things.

"Tell me again how you and Mia met? I don't think we talked about that either."

Juliet is now picking apart her barbecue sandwich and eating only the insides, leaving the bun at the side of the plate.

"She and I met in college—we lived next-door in the dorms. And then our sophomore year we became roommates, but still lived in the dorms because my parents wouldn't let me live in an apartment. She used to drag me out on Thursday nights to party; she can be credited for getting me out of my shell."

"You were in a shell?" I tease.

"Ha ha, very funny." Juliet rolls her eyes. "But yes, I'm not the most outgoing person you'll ever meet—I would consider myself more of an observer than anything else. Every once in a while I let my hair down and cut loose, but for the most part..." She shrugs.

It's true that she's not all that outgoing.

The side of her that leans more cautious toward strangers has definitely been gleaned by me; she was in no rush to welcome me with open arms the day we met. No rush to welcome Thad, either, which explains our presence here—although the douche has completely abandoned us.

"There's nothing wrong with being on the quiet side," I say, knowing full well that I'm the same way, too.

I've never been outgoing; not like my buddies, who shine in the spotlight.

Wracking my brain for something else to ask her, I chew on my barbeque, then nibble on the corn—I grabbed two cobs so I'm sure as shit gonna eat it though I'd rather talk than eat at the moment.

I want to know more about Juliet and for whatever reason...I want her to know more about me.

Weird, right?

Swallowing the corn in my mouth, I'm preparing something new to say when she beats me to it.

"What do you do exactly in finance, Davis?"

I rest my plate on my lap and use a napkin to wipe my fingers. "I'm in investments. It's not very exciting, but it pays the bills."

I want to roll my eyes at myself. *It's not very exciting, but it pays the bills?* I sound like a tool.

"How can you say it's not very exciting? I bet it has its moments and it's way more eventful than what I do for a living."

My ears perk up. "What is it you do?"

"I'm a teacher."

Is she being serious? "What grade?"

"Middle school English and social issues—sixth, seventh and eighth grade."

"Um—were you being sarcastic when you said me being in investments is more eventful than what you do because the last time I checked, middle schoolers are the literal worst."

Juliet tips her head back and lets out a laugh. "They have their moments, but for the most part they're respectful."

Pause. "Mostly." She lets out a long, drawn out sigh. "Okay fine, they're the worst, especially the boys because they're at the age where they're discovering what sex is and what certain things mean and sometimes it's a nightmare."

"How's that?"

She, too, puts down her plate to give me her full attention. "Well, for example, do you have any idea what it's like having to give a twelve-year-old boy detention because he is telling other students what a boner is in the middle of English class? Two weeks ago, I had to intervene during a discussion because this kid Evan was telling this kid Nick what sixty-nine-ing was. These boys have absolutely no self-control when it comes to word vomit and what's appropriate or not appropriate in class because they're just figuring out what all of this stuff means."

My mouth hangs open. "Stop it right now."

Juliet nods enthusiastically. "Question: Do you want to talk about things that make a grown woman blush? The answer is: twelve- year-old boys."

"That shit does not happen in middle school, does it? How are these kids so..." I search for the right words.

"Perverted?" she supplies. "The internet. Television. Video games. Social media—do you need me to list more reasons? Kids these days are nothing like we were, they're growing up so fast. Way *way* too fast. It's terrifying. No one wants to over-hear a student say the word cocksucker during an English class. Or ask what it is. God, it's a nightmare sometimes."

"You actually give detentions for that?"

She shrugs. "Sure—they know it's inappropriate. Some-times they'll go as far as googling things right then and there, and they're not supposed to have their phones in class. Basi-cally, being a middle school teacher in this day and age isn't for the faint of heart."

"Would you care to retract your statement about it being un-eventful?"

Juliet nods. "I probably should, shouldn't I?"

"Yeah—I have a desk job, more or less. Lots of being on the computer, watching stocks and reading legal documents. It's mind numbing most days."

Unless I watch porn or something...

Or exercise.

"You're shaping the youth of America."

"I'm teaching them how to form sentences which they only seem to use for posting on TikTok." She sighs again heavily, digging her fork into the food on her plate. "It's a vicious cycle."

She's so cute when she's morose, shoulders slumped.

Ben is walking around with cans of White Claw and Juliet takes one, giving me a side-eye. "I'm only going to have one, cross my heart and swear to die."

"Good, because I don't want any repeats of last night."

"I'm sorry you had to babysit me, it is not your job." Juliet hesitates. "Actually, it's no one's job, ha ha."

There she is, dropping hints that she's single. Was that a hint for me, or just a jab at herself? So hard to know.

I change the subject. "So you're a teacher, who wants a dog, but lives in an apartment. What else is there to know about you? What's the last trip you took, not including this one?"

It doesn't take her long to ponder this question. "My parents' anniversary, we went on a cruise to the Caribbean—which was two years ago. I like to keep it local."

"Do you?"

"Um *no*. I'm just saying that because I never get to go anywhere."

I smile at her while she sips from her adult seltzer beverage. Never had a taste for those things, they're basically flavored water and I need at least five to feel any effects, which is a lot of effort for a buzz.

I stick to beer tonight.

Pop the top of one when Ben hands it to me and sip off the foam.

"What's the last trip you took?" Juliet wants to know, pulling apart the brownie on her plate and biting into it with her front teeth.

I watch, mesmerized. "I uh..." I clear my throat. "Went to the Bahamas for a wedding in June and Vegas for a trade show, and I was in Nashville two weeks ago for my buddy's baby shower."

Juliet looks impressed. "All of that this year?"

"Yeah, I get around."

We laugh and then go silent again, the mood shifting.

"Favorite food?" I blurt out.

"Steak and a baked potato."

I nod approvingly; it's a great answer mainly because I too love a good steak and baked potato, none of which we've eaten over the course of our stay here.

"Yours?"

"I would have said the same thing, so I'll also add a good cheeseburger and fries. Or seafood—love me some seafood."

Juliet hides her smile. "You're a carnivore through and through, hey?"

"I guess? But I also love dessert, and nuts, and desserts with nuts."

"So nuts but especially nuts in your dessert."

She smirks.

I stare blankly at her. Was she just making an innuendo about balls being in my food?

It's hard to tell, she has a neutral expression and hasn't made a single suggestive comment for the thirty-six plus hours I've known her.

She blinks up at me. "What?"

"Did you just..."

Juliet tilts her head. "Did I just what?" Takes a small bite of brownie, grinning with food on her teeth.

"Nevermind."

She laughs, wiping the corners of her mouth with a napkin. "Oh my god, Davis, you should see your face. Too funny."

So she was making an innuendo, the little shit! "Why you little pervert."

She lifts her shoulders in a shrug. "Maybe I learn a thing or two from my students, maybe not."

"Are you saying you're basically a twelve-year-old boy?"

"I mean..." She examines the fingers on her right hand. "If the shoe fits."

"It must be hard keeping that inside."

Juliet pauses. "That's what she said."

Oh my god.

I stare at her again. "What the hell happened to you?" Is she always like this?

I have so many questions now that will probably remain unanswered.

"What do you mean, what happened to me?"

"You were being so..."

"Polite?" She rolls her eyes. "Duh, I didn't know you."

Huh. Interesting.

"Are you into any sports?"

"Are you asking if I like watching football for hours on the couch on Sunday and Monday?"

That makes me laugh, but also: "Yes?"

She shrugs. "Depends on what food is being served but mostly no. I don't enjoy sitting around on the weekends mindlessly watching football on television, no offense."

"Hockey? Baseball? Basketball?"

"If I had to choose, I'd pick hockey—but not on TV."

Hmm.

"Do you play any sports?"

She tilts her head, takes a sip of her drink and thinks as she swallows. "Why do men always ask if women play sports? It's not like I'm chasing around trying to be a quarterback. Or playing soccer in the park."

"I guess I'm just asking if you're athletic."

"Sure. I won't pass up a game of pool badminton if you wanted to play, but as you could probably tell, I cannot fish."

"What's pool badminton?"

"Haven't you ever heard of badminton?"

"Yes, but...in the pool?"

"Let's see, how do I describe it." She taps her chin. "It's badminton but...in the pool. The best part is when you're short and you're in the deep end and you're trying not to drown as your nephew lobs the birdie in your face."

Ahh, so she has a nephew, which means she's not an only child.

"Would you consider yourself competitive?"

"Gosh no, I don't think so? I mean, if you win a game I will congratulate you. Definitely not a sore loser, I'm genuinely happy for my friends when they accomplish something and since we're on the subject, I'm happy for my friend's happiness."

Her eyes drift to her best friend, who is sitting on my best friend's lap. They look cozy—like they'd rather be holed up in their fancy, boho decorated tent.

Damn, Thad is into her.

He's got his fingers running through her hair and for a brief moment I wonder if they've ever gotten caught in her weave.

"Do you think he's ever pulled the extensions out of her head?" I muse quietly so only Juliet can hear me.

"Actually yeah—he has."

It surprises me that he's never told me this. It seems like we'd have gotten a good laugh out of the mishap.

Guess he doesn't kiss and tell after all, although he did tell me about the first time they slept together; the sparks, how great it was. Gag.

"He has?"

"Yes and she was mortified," Juliet laughs. "I think he learned his lesson after that—keep your fingers out of her scalp."

I laugh. "Has anyone ever gotten their fingers stuck in your extensions?" My eyes go to her long, dark hair.

"Um no—I don't have extensions." She sounds slightly put out by the suggestion.

"That's your hair?"

"*Yes* it's my hair," she tells me with a tone that clearly says 'duh, you moron.'

I want to touch it so I lean over and slide my hand through the brown tresses. It's silky like a waterfall.

Soft as soft can be.

Juliet rears away from me, holding up her can of White Claw and her plate of food. "Okay buddy, lay off the alcohol."

"I'm not drunk. It's one beer and I haven't even had half of it yet."

That gives her pause. "Are you a half full or half empty kind of guy?"

"Definitely half full." I don't even have to think twice about my response. "I'd say I'm...annoyingly optimistic. Eternal optimist. I shun pessimism."

Which would explain why Willa was able to gaslight me for so damn long.

Ugh.

I'm too trusting and nice, dammit!

"I can totally see that about you," Juliet says, lowering her plate. "And you can touch my hair, you just caught me off guard, that's all. I'm not used to men...you know. Being nice."

"Is that why you just assumed Thad was a player and I, guilty by association?"

She nods. "One hundred percent. The last few guys I went out with were all wrong, for the wrong reasons—just a bunch of assholes who didn't deserve me."

Juliet seems to know her self-worth.

It took me a few years to know mine. I had to learn it all over again; seems she and I are no different in that regard.

We finish off our dinners; when Juliet is left with an empty plate I rise from my chair, extending my hand as an offering to take hers to the trash. She hands it to me, smile on her face—and if I'm not mistaken, her eyes do a quick scan down the front of my body.

She's hiding the perusal well but...there it is.

I grab us two bottles of water while I'm up, returning to the fire and my chair, setting them both down on the ground. Reaching forward I snatch up everything we need for a little bit of sweets; some s'mores. Considering she barfed up the one she had last night, I'm not quite sure she'll be in the mood to smell or taste them—but I definitely am. I could eat chocolate every single night of the week.

While I am loading the stick with marshmallows, I glance at Juliet over my shoulder to find her watching me intently.

"Want one?"

She nods, taking the marshmallow from my stick, slowly prying it off as it oozes and goos, blowing on it before opening her mouth to taste it.

"Yummy."

"Damn right it's yummy—I'm famous for my mallow browning skills."

Her brow cocks. "Famous? Surely that's an exaggeration."

"He is," Thad interjects, the sneaky eavesdropper

appearing out of nowhere. "Once, at Training Camp, he made his famous apple pie for everyone. From scratch."

"You bake?" Mia asks from her perch on my best friend's lap. Huh. They must have moved their chairs closer when I wasn't paying attention. At least, not to them.

"Some. Not very often," I demure, which is a lie. I cook and bake all the time—for Penelope and Skipper, obviously. I haven't mastered the art of quantities and always over-make, left with a ton of food and since the pair of them are in the house next door...

We eat together a lot.

Like, a lot a lot.

"He's being modest." Thad leans forward and gives me a bump on the upper bicep with his fist. "Baked chicken—that was a good meal."

I poke at the fire with my stick. "Yeah, I make good baked chicken."

Big whoop, my tone seems to say.

"And you're a wonder with the slow cooker."

"Stop, you're making me blush." I swat a hand in the air. "Anyone can use a slow cooker."

"But your recipes are like magic," Thad tells me, more to Juliet than anyone and I get what he's trying to do: make me look good.

It seems to be working because she's watching me again, head cocked, slowly licking the marshmallow off her fingers, and I highly doubt she's trying to look suggestive but that's how it's coming off and I'm here for it.

Er.

I glance away, not wanting to be caught staring.

"Do you cook?" I ask, eating the remaining mallows on my stick—there are two, and I pick at them slowly to allow Juliet time to answer.

"Not really. It's just me, so..." Her shoulders move up and down in a shrug.

"Yeah, the last time you cooked me dinner I was sick for two days," Mia jokes, earning a scowl from her boyfriend. If she's trying to play matchmaker and point out her bestie's positive traits, that was a fail. "And didn't you take that cooking class at Le Cordon Bleu so you wouldn't kill people?"

Her nose goes up. "You had the flu—it was an unlucky coincidence."

She sounds indignant and rightfully so.

Mia is nitpicking.

"You're probably right," Mia amends. "It wasn't the half raw chicken that made me sick, it was the flu."

Thad feigns a gag, retching over his chair, and they both laugh.

"Ha ha," Juliet laments with an eye roll. "I never claimed to be a chef; I do what I gotta do to stay alive."

We all laugh at that.

She's cute.

"What she lacks in the kitchen she makes up for on the slopes," Mia supplies, doing her best to turn the conversation around. "Juliet is a great skier."

"Skiing? She only mentioned pool badminton as a sport," I tell the duo, who have gone back to canoodling, feeding each other fireside snacks and peppering each other with kisses.

"Do you ski?" Juliet asks.

"No—I snowboard, sort of. Not well, but I get by." Actually, I fall a lot but I'm not about to admit that. It's not as if she's ever going to see me on the slopes. "Are you any good?"

"I suppose? I joined the ski team when I was in middle school because I had a crush on this kid, Jack—and he was on the ski team. Anything I could do to maximize my stalking," she laughs. "Even joined the soccer team, too. He did both."

"And how did that work out?"

"It didn't. I quit the ski team after I got stuck under the toll rope one night, the coach was shouting at me so loud. I was totally humiliated, being what—thirteen? Never went back after that, although I did continue to ski. And play soccer."

"You took up two sports just so you could impress a boy?"

"Hey man, I was an idiot, okay? It took me a long ass time to realize I needed to live for myself and not try to please or impress other people. Especially men." There is a pine cone beneath her chair and she retrieves it from the ground, picking at its seeds, pulling them off one by one.

"There's nothing idiotic about wanting to please or impress other people. The important thing is you eventually learned that you need to come first. It took me a really long time to realize that; mainly it took getting screwed over by the woman I was living with for me to realize what a dumbass I was being. I wouldn't call myself a pushover exactly, but I was pretty blind for a really long time."

I have no idea why I'm telling her all this, especially with the peanut gallery sitting a mere three feet away, no doubt listening to every word I'm saying. I'm sure Thad will have an opinion for me later; my buddy will have zero qualms telling me what he thinks about my little speech and the fact that I'm opening up to Juliet in a group setting.

Ugh, fuck my life.

When it comes to gossip and shit, Thad is horrible.

Loves repeating shit, loves being in the center of it, though he'll deny liking drama, he seems to be surrounded by it, current girlfriend notwithstanding.

Regardless. I wish I'd kept my mouth shut with Thad nearby taking mental notes.

Juliet shifts in her seat, still picking away at the pine cone, eyes darting between Thad, Mia and myself—I can see she wants to say more but instead, presses her lips together.

Hides a smile.

The fire crackles, sparks glowing in the pitch-black night. Everyone around the fire is quiet tonight, enjoying the calm. I'm assuming we are the only four leaving in the morning considering this parcel arrived later than we did. Several conversations are happening at once; Lionel and Suzanne have their heads pressed together and are laughing about something quietly. Steve and Paul are both sipping on beer, holding hands.

Erik and Cookie are also canoodling, but in that weird, conniving looking way that gave me the skeeves on my first night here.

What was it Juliet said about them? That they're probably definitely swingers?

I shrink back, not wanting to appear too friendly, grateful they haven't approached me to bang them. I'm not the three-some or foursome type, thank you very much.

"I know what you're thinking."

Beside me, Juliet has put down the pine cone and has the White Claw back in her hand.

"What am I thinking?"

She moves closer, lowering her voice. "You're thinking...it was probably Cookie outside the camper last night coming to get you."

"Pfft. It hadn't crossed my mind." I pause to add, "Wait. You were trashed, how do you remember anything about last night?"

"Eh, once I throw up I'm usually fine—not that I get drunk all the time, because I don't. The last time I threw up from drinking was probably college." She sips on her drink. "Anyways, she's definitely interested."

"Would you be quiet? They're old enough to be our parents."

Juliet laughs. "Oh come on, don't be so dramatic and stop playing so hard to get."

"Listen—all I can tell you is I'm really fucking glad we're leaving tomorrow. I feel like they're working up their courage to come over here, so she can fondle my nut sac."

Juliet's eyes widen. "You have a high opinion of yourself! Maybe they want to come over here so he can cop a feel of my boobs."

"Doubtful. It's me they're after."

When she laughs, it's so loud the entire group stops what they're doing to look over.

"Would you like to share with the rest of the class what you find so funny?" Lionel asks, his hand sliding over his wife's knee.

"Sorry—I had something caught in the back of my throat."

And it wasn't my dick.

I laugh at my own private joke, joining her, the pair of us idiotically giggling like two fools.

"Poor you, you're so sexy that older women are lusting after you in front of their husbands. Boo hoo."

"Did you just call me sexy?" First she admits she thinks I'm good-looking, now she's admitting she thinks I'm sexy?

Woohoo!!!

She groans. "Ugh—here we go again, stop quoting me. I was being facetious."

"Eh? Try not using such big words."

"I was being flippant. Joking. Teasing."

"Liar." I settle back into my chair, confident she finds me attractive, all is right with the world.

And tonight, she's not drunk and I won't have to babysit her back to the camper, which makes the evening that much better. Perhaps tonight I'll get a good night's rest.

Not likely on that deplorable bed, but a guy can dream.

"You're calling me a liar? How do you know you're even my type—some people may not be into you." Her eyes give me another once-over. "What you've got going on here."

"What I've got going on here?" I repeat. "What exactly is it you think I've got going on?" Seriously, I want to know.

"Stop fishing for compliments, it's beneath you."

"No seriously, what is it you think I've got going on?" Because I haven't shaved in three days, I'm wearing the same jeans, and my pits probably reek like the garlic from the barbeque sauce.

CHAPTER 7
Juliet

"For pity's sake, Davis—cut the false modesty act."

"False modesty? I'm as humble as they come."

Obviously I don't believe him; men as good-looking as Davis couldn't *possibly* be modest, could they? I've certainly never met a man who was even half this attractive who wasn't an arrogant prick.

Could Davis possess all the qualities of the perfect man as if he were created especially for me and dropped down in the middle of the woods?

Funny, kind, giving.

Tall, dark, handsome.

Stronger than strong.

Burly, even.

Even his five o'clock shadow is doing it for me in a big way and I normally don't go for stubble on a man; usually love a freshly shaved jawline given that I'm anti-beard burn.

Ha!

Dream on, Juliet.

I have an idea. "How about *you* describe *yourself* to me instead."

His eyes dart to Thad and Mia, who have long given up on us as entertainment for the evening. In fact, I can hear them whispering about sneaking off, wondering if I'll be fine here with Davis, so they can spend their last night screwing their brains out buck naked in the woods as God intended.

Oy vey.

"You want me to tell you what I've got going on here?" He gestures up and down his own body, beer bottle in his large, strong hand.

"Sure. Go for it."

He's quiet a few moments as he gathers his thoughts. "Alright, well. Let's see...who am I, who am I..." His head tilts back, resting on the back of the chair as he gazes up at the sky, avoiding direct eye contact. "Okay, If I were to build a profile on a dating site, this is what I might say to describe myself."

I wait.

"Tall, hardworking man who values family. Good communicator. Honest." Davis pauses again to think, finally turning his face to look at me. "I live with intention."

"You live with intention? What does that even mean?"

"Yes, I mean what I do, and do what I say I'm going to do. I don't talk just to hear the sound of my own voice. Conflict isn't necessary and can be avoided. I..." He clears his throat. "When I say and do things, they are for a purpose. I'm trying to make the world a better place. So what if my face cleans up good and I'm okay to look at when I'm wearing a dress shirt? Is that going to help anyone?"

I'm doing everything I can to keep my mouth from dropping open and falling on the damn ground.

I want to grab his hand and drag him out of the campground and have my way with him, or is that this baby bit of alcohol talking?

"Look, if you meet enough pretty people and discover they're only pretty on the outside, it doesn't take long to learn none of that shit matters. Not that I don't appreciate a beautiful woman because I do—you're gorgeous—"

My stomach flutters.

"—but beauty doesn't make someone faithful. Or a loyal friend. Or a good mother." His lips purse; he resembles an old woman who's tasted a lemon. "So I'm tall, big whoop and sure, I have big muscles." He flexes his bicep. "And so what if I speak three different languages fluently?"

My brows shoot into my hairline. "You can?"

"*Oui.*"

Oh brother, this guy.

I choke back a giggle. "Is that your dating profile bio? It's very wordy."

He glances at me again, irritated. "I was being sincere."

"I'm sorry—I don't know why that made me uncomfortable because you're one hundred percent correct. I guess I'm just very...surprised. And taken aback by you." I fiddle with the can in my hands, pulling at the pop top. "I came on this trip prepared to not like you, or Thad, and you're both perfectly agreeable."

"Perfectly agreeable?" He scoffs. "Come on, Juliet, you're an English teacher, surely you can do better than that."

I smile, catching my lower lip between my teeth. "Fine, Thad is agreeable—he's not awful, I can tolerate him."

"And me? Am I tolerable?"

He knows he is, the brat. "You're...nice."

For a heartbeat, neither of us say a word.

Then.

"You did not just call me nice!" he booms with a laugh, leaning to snatch up the s'mores making utensils, loading the stick with more marshmallows—four—and holding it above the fire. "Nice. Never in my fucking life has anyone called me nice," he grumbles with a laugh. "I made you dessert! I tucked you in bed! I held your hair back!"

"*So* nice," I tease.

"Buddy, are you hearing this? Juliet thinks I'm nice."

Thad nods. "You *are* nice."

"Yeah but..." He leans closer to the fire, its embers burning low, a sure signal that the evening will soon be coming to an end.

Closer still.

"Shit!" Davis screeches. "Damn, that burns!"

He remains crouched, nursing his mallows and his butt hurt feelings and my stomach dances knowing he'll share the sweet treats with me.

"Bro, you scream like a gi—"

Thad stops talking when Davis turns, rising to his full height before plopping back down in his chair.

Davis stops plucking at the charred marshmallows. "What?"

"Bro." Thad points in his face, sticking his finger on Davis's forehead.

It gets swatted away. "Dude, stop touching me."

Oh lord. *Lordy, lordy, lordy.*

I chug the rest of my drink, swallow and wipe my mouth before saying, "Davis, I don't know how to delicately put this, so I'm just going to give it to you straight. Your eye—"

"Your fucking eyebrow is gone, Halbrook!" Thad shouts. "Fucking. *Gone.*"

Davis laughs as if Thad were telling a hilarious joke, pulling the end marshmallow off his stick and holding it for me to take.

"Want some?"

"Um," I stutter, willing myself not to laugh. "Um. Your, um..."

"What's wrong with you? Why are you staring at me like that?"

Thad slaps him merrily on the back. "You singed your fucking eyebrow off, bro! How drunk are you?"

Davis shakes his head vigorously in protest. "No I did not."

"You did." He reaches in his back pocket and pulls out his phone, thrusting it in his friend's direction. "Look."

Thad holds the camera app open so Davis is able to get a good, long look at himself: two eyes, one nose, one mouth.

One eyebrow.

"No." He feels around his face with the tip of his fingers. "What the fuck! I'm not drunk at all!"

Thad cracks up. "You look so stupid right now, man. Holy shit, let me get a picture of this."

"Shut up, asshole!"

"I'm not the moron who burnt off his facial hair." He reaches up again to run his fingers along Davis's face, but a quick swipe of the hand knocks it away.

"Stop touching me! Just stop."

In her chair, Mia is hiding her laugh, face buried in a hooded sweatshirt she's holding in her arms, shoulders shaking.

"Can I please take your picture?" Thad has the balls to ask.

"No one is taking my picture!" He glances at me and my eyes go wide. So wide I probably look as if I've seen a ghost or something shocking.

"You have to let me." Thad is going on and on. "This is too goddamn good."

"Remind me why we're friends again?" Davis's voice is sullen and pouty. "I hate you right now."

"You're just saying that because you feel stupid—but you look stupid, so your feelings are valid."

"Shut up." He's still pouting and I don't blame him: this is not a good look for him.

SARA NEY

"Don't say shut up, it's rude," his best friend chastises, making the situation worse.

I study his profile.

I've never actually seen anyone who is missing their eyebrow before unless it was in the movies. I'm tempted to touch it too but I know it would piss him off even more, plus, it's probably sore from the fire.

I laugh at the thought but cover my mouth, hoping he doesn't notice.

Oh my god, unreal.

Too funny.

When a snort escapes my nose, his head whips around— but the expression on his face, coupled with the...*lack* of hair above his brow...makes me bust out laughing.

"Do you smell that?" Thad asks. "It's like... burnt hair."

Davis looks agitated. "Did I not tell you to be quiet?"

His best friend raises his arms in a mocking shrug. "Hey, don't shoot the messenger—the one brow makes you look like a pirate. And now you don't need that brow lift to look younger because you look more youthful and... surprised."

We're all dying now, laughing and laughing harder when Thad sneaks a few photos to post on the internet when the cell reception is better.

We laugh harder still when he storms out of the campfire and onto the path, disappearing into the night.

CHAPTER 8
Davis

I'm in the bathroom inspecting my face when Juliet graces me with her presence, obsessed with the hairless area above my left eye, pressing into the skin where it was singed.

How could I not feel the heat burning my flesh when I was browning that fucking marshmallow?

Idiot.

I am a freaking idiot.

I raise my brows, wishing there was better lighting in this tiny space, leaning as close to the mirror as I can get, fingers gingerly touching the tender mound above my eye.

"The hairless, tender mound." I chuckle to myself.

"That sounds porny." Juliet has a smug smile on her face as she appears in the door I kept open.

"That did, didn't it."

"Quiet." Her eyes roam from my mouth to my nose to my forehead, focused on that bald part of me. "Honestly, you're kind of too cute with one eyebrow and when you're mad. I'm tempted to kiss your brow and make it better."

I can't tell if she's joking about either of those things.

"If having my face temporarily jacked up turns you on,

then you can have at it." I pucker my lips, still watching my own reflection in the mirror.

Juliet crosses her arms as she leans against the doorway, shoulder against the fake wood trim.

"Why'd you run off like that earlier?"

"Um, I don't know if you noticed, but I'm a social pariah now."

"That's a bit dramatic even for you." She lifts a hand to scratch at her nose. "Thad and the rest of them were just teasing. I mean—they care you got hurt, but your hair will grow back."

"Excuse me for not wanting to stand around listening to strangers laughing at my expense."

Not into it.

Juliet nods slowly. "I get that, I do. But we leave tomorrow and the fun didn't have to be over."

"The fun was over the minute I lit my face on fire." I point to my ear. "And got hooked in the ear. How much more can this body take?"

Let's not forget the animals that have been sniffing around outside when the sun goes down.

"Are you ever going to let me live down 'the hooking'?"

The hooking.

Ha ha.

"Obviously." I study my face again. "Doubt I'll run into you much after this weekend, so you're safe from the nonstop jabs."

"Fair enough." She yawns now, lifting her arms above her head as she does so, the sweatshirt she's wearing lifts—it's not midriff baring but I get a nice little view of her hips and stomach.

Juliet glances behind her into the kitchen, where I've already assembled the "bed" I'll be sleeping on again tonight.

It looks so bloody uncomfortable I visibly wince just looking at it.

I've never been more relieved to be leaving a "vacation" in all my life. In fact, I'll be taking a vacation from this one as soon as it can be arranged. Aruba, perhaps. Or Cabo? That sounds like a goddamn delight.

"I'm going to get my jammers on," Juliet tells me by way of stepping back from the door, closing it slightly so she can squeeze past and into her bedroom. I hear her rooting around her suitcase before it goes quiet; she's likely pulling on some pants and a sweatshirt.

I wrap up this staring contest I'm having with myself so she can use the toilet and the mirror, too—brush her teeth and do whatever she's got to do—miserably making my way to the cot in the kitchen.

Nothing to do, but climb on.

Grunting, I shift, doing my best to find a comfy spot.

I roll to my right side, feet hanging off the end a good, solid foot, which means my feet are ripe for the picking from any boogeymen or monsters lingering in the dark.

Lord, why am I like this?

I'm a grown-ass man who is still afraid of the dark.

Shivering, I pull the tissue up over my shoulders.

Roll to my other side, fluffing the wadded-up clothes that have become my pillow because I hadn't wanted an argument from my roommate by asking to borrow one of hers.

She'd give you one if you bothered to ask, she's not an asshole.

It's one night—you survived Hell Week during football training camp, you can survive one night in a camper with shitty bedding.

I continue telling this to myself as I lay here, flipping to my back after I can't settle in on my side.

Sigh loudly.

Stare at the ceiling a good three minutes before sighing again and rolling back to my left.

"How's it going in there?" Juliet shouts from the small bedroom, oblivious to my plight no more.

"Fine," I lie.

"You don't sound fine."

That's because I'm lying on a board with only a thin blanket to warm me, thanks for caring.

"I am."

Juliet is quiet for a few seconds before I hear her soft laughter. "You know, that's what my students always say when I ask ,but they're usually fibbing because they feel embarrassed I'm asking."

"I'm not embarrassed. I just...can't sleep."

Not only am I extremely sore, stiff, and cold, it's impossible for me to train my ears from listening to the whistling wind and sounds from outside.

"Anything I can do to help?"

Yeah—you can let me on my half of that bed.

"No, we're good."

"You sure? Do you want a bedtime story?"

That makes me smile in the dark, Juliet sitting on the end of my bed telling me a story to make me sleepy.

Won't work, but cute idea.

"Ha."

We're both silent after that and eventually I go back to staring at the ceiling, listening, thinking, mind filled with all kinds of random thoughts.

Wishing Juliet and I had connected sooner rather than finding our middle ground today.

Why had we not met sooner—why had Thad and Mia not introduced us before this weekend?

I like her.

Am attracted to her.

She's cute and funny and smart.

A teacher? Yes please. *Not* that I have a fetish or anything, but the idea of her molding young minds turns me on in a way that wouldn't turn me on if she were an accountant or an architect or something.

She's a bit bossy and I like it.

After I'm lying here a while, there's a rustling sound from the other room and the bedroom door slides open.

I can't see Juliet but I obviously hear her when she asks, "Davis? Are you awake?"

Uh, duh—I'm lying on a table and I have to be up for the airport in a few hours. "Yeah, I'm awake."

"Did you hear that noise?"

I crane my ear, listening. "What was it?"

Her feet shuffle. "I don't know—sounded like sticks breaking but nearby? Do you think someone is out there?"

Someone—or someTHING.

I swallow, trying to be brave. "I'm sure it's nothing but the wind..." *Says everyone in every horror movie before they go get themselves murdered.*

Crash.

Juliet

"WHAT WAS THAT?" I'M DEFINITELY NOT GOING TO be able to sleep tonight if I keep hearing strange sounds outside the camper and not know what it is that's making it.

I walk over to the bathroom and flip on the little light, not wanting to illuminate the entire interior ,but wanting to see where I'm going.

"You heard that too?" Davis's eyes are wide and he looks

terrified, sitting up now and is it just me or is he clutching that blanket to his chest?

"I'm not sure what you think you heard, but I heard what sounded like cans maybe? But there are no garbage cans outside?" It's a statement and a question, both at the same time, curiosity has me walking through the camper and to the little front door.

"You are not going out there!" Davis tells me, anchored to his spot.

"I heard something but it's probably nothing but the wind, chill out." I glance at him over my shoulder as his eyes dart into the woods, his one missing eyebrow looking decidedly ridiculous without its matching pair. "Why do you look like you've just pissed your pants?"

"Because I *am* pissing my pants." He sounds mildly disgruntled.

"You're funny." And cute.

I laugh, unlocking the screen so I can open the other one.

"Don't open that, are you insane?" Davis hasn't moved from his spot on the bed—or table, whatever that is he has to sleep on, poor bastard. Looks dreadfully uncomfortable.

A twinge of guilt tingles in my belly.

"Are you sure it was nothing? It's pitch-black out there and I feel something watching us."

He can't even see out the windows with his head buried in a blanket, the giant goof.

I roll my eyes, but let them stray to the dark tree line, the trail we take during the day with zero hesitations appearing incredibly foreboding at night.

I shiver, shrugging Davis's hands off me. "Wait. Did you just pull me in front of you as protection?"

"No."

He looks guilty as all hell.

"Oh my god—you were going to use my body as a shield against bears!"

"No I wasn't!" He pauses. "Besides, a bear can go right through you—you're as flimsy as a sheet of paper as far as defense mechanisms."

I smack him. "You're horrible, do you know that? Horrible! I'm glad you only have one eyebrow—serves you right!"

Davis begins laughing, tipping his head back, the deep chuckle causes all my best girl parts to flutter.

"But seriously, Juliet, I am begging you not to open the door. Please."

He sounds so earnest and sincere that I turn to look at him; and now that I'm giving him a closer inspection, I can see that he's well and truly terrified.

"Davis, are you afraid of what's outside?"

"No." He hesitates far too long for that 'no' to be sincere. "Well, only if it's like a bear or something that can eat me."

"Are you afraid of *bears*?"

He shrugs, neither confirming or denying, though I suppose his nonverbals are confirmation enough and his fear would explain a lot about the way he's acting.

Hmmm.

I look him over. "You know I'm here to protect you, right?"

I tease him in an attempt to lighten the mood, flexing my bicep. The gesture is humorous because he is so much bigger than I am, although I am so much braver.

Honestly, I'm a bit shocked he's freaking out like this.

Never in a million years would I have pegged him for a guy that would have this kind of irrational fear. Not that I am judging him, I'm surprised, that's all.

He's afraid of something that is never going to hurt him, yet he is afraid regardless.

It's not for me to say the fear is ridiculous, the same way he can't tell me I shouldn't be terrified of snakes. Or heights. I'm fine flying, but try to drive me across a bridge?

I turn into a blubbering idiot.

"My god, I'm so tired—I haven't slept at all in the past few days."

I nod to show my understanding. "Well you had a long day. You spent it hiding from Erik and Cookie, fried off your brow hair, now you've got bears lurking outside."

Sucks to be him.

Davis draws in a breath, holds it a few seconds before letting it go.

"*Pleaseletmesleepwithyou*, Juliet," he rattles off quickly, sounding like a kid. "I need thicker blankets, so I can hide and that protection you offered."

"You're absolutely ridiculous."

"I'm begging you." He folds his hands together in mock prayer, beseeching me so I'll let him in the big bed and not make him sleep on the kitchen foldout table slash bed where he's susceptible to attack.

"Honestly, I feel drunk with power."

His face contorts. "I hate to bring this up but technically it would be my turn for the big bed since we're sharing the camper and all, and neither one of us is paying for it. Wouldn't etiquette dictate that we rotate every other night, ergo, this would be my night for the bedroom?"

Shit.

He's right.

"It's like that, is it?"

His chin nods. "Is it?"

A better human would concede to him because he's absolutely right; I should one hundred percent sleep in the main living space tonight so he gets a good night's sleep. After all, he has to be awake at the ass crack of dawn (or before that) and the foldout bed (if we can call it that) is hardly fit for a man of his size.

He hasn't said anything about it, but I'd wager he doesn't fit on it. Like, at all.

However, I am not a better person.

I am the person who thought they were going to be in the Caribbean sipping on island punch and laying in a swaying hammock between two palm trees—but that's neither here nor there.

I am the person who also enjoys decent shut eye and REM sleep and not waking to a stiff back.

The reality is: I'm marooned in the woods, in a small glamper with a strange dude I've only just met (granted, he's a cute dude); if I don't want him to think I'm a complete shrew, I will give up and not argue.

However, I am also the human who would much rather share the big bed than sleep out in the living space and lose any sleep at all from being uncomfortable.

"I can't even take you seriously right now." I busy myself by folding and refolding the hand towel resting on the tiny kitchen counter, loud clanging outside our camper only growing louder.

Or closer.

Davis moves closer, too.

He really is scared and doesn't bother hiding it.

Taking pity on us both, I relent with a resigned sigh. "Okay Davis, you can sleep in the bedroom with me."

It's all the invitation he needs.

He snatches up his little blanket, making a quick beeline for the bedroom at the back of the camper, barely missing a step and practically flying through the air as fear propels him.

His feet barely touch the ground when he flies onto the mattress.

With a roll of my eyes, I move to close and lock the screen

door, remembering to turn off the bathroom light on my way past, basically shutting down the camper all over again for our second attempt at bedtime.

I find Davis sitting on the right side when I make it back to the bedroom; he hasn't gotten under the covers yet, watching me enter the doorway, gesturing to the right side then the left.

"I wasn't sure which side you wanted me on."

I shrug, nerves fluttering in my stomach. "Whichever side is fine, I can sleep on either, it doesn't matter."

He nods again before folding back the covers on the side he's already on, sliding his legs under. At least, that's what it seems like he's doing—I can only see his silhouette in the dark, listen to the sound of the rustling sheets.

It feels foreign climbing into bed beside him, but my heart is racing at the same time, excited.

This *feels* exciting.

I've been thinking about his lips and his eyes and how tall he is all damn weekend, this enigma of a man I was prepared to hate but don't dislike at all, not even a little, and now I'm climbing into bed with him.

So what if he currently only has one eyebrow, he's still fucking gorgeous.

How on earth will I ever sleep?

Outside, there is more noise, but this time I'm convinced it's rattling from the wind and nothing more.

Davis doesn't concur, scooching across the bed to be comforted until our shoulders touch.

"Oh my god—hold me."

He's now encroaching on my side faster than I can flip a light switch.

I can't stop the nervous laughter bubbling out of me. "You're not being serious right now."

I don't mind him wanting to be enveloped in a hug or held; not the least or even a little bit.

"I am." With the sliver of light shining through the narrow bedroom window, I see that his eyes are wide and terrified. "If I had a woobie or a blanket right now I'd be sucking my thumb." The laugh is punctuated by trembling and I feel a pang of sympathy for the poor guy.

Instead of sounding concerned, however, I ask, "What the hell is a woobie?"

I feel Davis shrugging closely beside me. "A blanket. The yellow blanket I used to carry around when I was little—it had a rabbit head and it was my best friend."

Aww. "Sounds like Linus from Snoopy."

"Kind of. Never sucked my thumb, though I'm tempted to do it right now." Davis laughs, his tone a bit less harried.

More calm.

"Hate to break it to you, Big Guy, but there's no way I could protect you if an animal got through that door unless it was a squirrel, and even then, there's a chance I'd be useless."

Also: squirrels are pure evil out to take over the world and everyone knows it.

Everyone.

If you don't think squirrels are out to get us, you're a liar.

In fact, when I was in college our campus was littered with the beady eyed cretins; they would stare me down on my walk to class and I dreaded the day one decided he wanted to nest in my long hair.

Shudder

I relax, settling in, pulling the covers up and laying on my back staring at the ceiling as I'd done the night before; Davis does the same.

"Know what's weird?" he asks into the dark.

"What?"

"Now that you mention squirrels, I don't remember seeing any outside during the day. Isn't that weird?"

That *is* weird and now that I'm thinking about it—he's

right. I haven't seen many squirrels. "You would think they'd be everywhere since this is nature and all."

Davis is quiet. Then, "Probably hiding out and waiting to strike."

Ha! "Are you one of those people who believes they're out to take over the world?"

"I'd call it a hostile takeover—those little bastards can't be trusted."

I nod. "I totally agree."

"See, we do have a lot in common," he tells me. "You like sleep, I like sleep. You don't like squirrels, I don't like squirrels."

That assessment makes me laugh. "I hope that's not where the similarities end—hating squirrels isn't a commonality I'd brag about."

"True."

Beside me, Davis shifts his large body, our legs knocking together as he tries to get comfortable.

"Sorry."

I smile in the dark. "Don't apologize."

Something about the circumstances of tonight—the humor of Davis singeing his eyebrows off, how funny it is that he feels security being near me when he thinks there are bears outside ready to attack him (as if I could save us), being here in the woods, being secluded... it all has me feeling a certain kind of way.

Softer? More affectionate?

I can't put my finger on the thoughts going through my head or the flutters that are in my stomach, but when Davis's hand hits the mattress and rests between our two bodies, I find my hand gravitating toward it.

Slowly I slide my palm over his, a tingling jolt of electricity shooting up my arm, down my spine, and throughout my entire body.

What is this?

He's not a stranger anymore. He's not really my friend; not really, not so soon. Can that happen this soon? Friendship?

We're certainly absolutely not *dating*. This wasn't a setup in any way by our friends, I'm sure of it. *So why do I suddenly feel romantic right now?*

Why do I want something to happen between us?

I'm not normally this kind of girl—but then, I've never been stranded with a man in a camper before. Seems my imagination takes me to places I don't normally go when I'm in close quarters with a dick.

My hand lingers over his.

His arm twitches as if the motion tickles him.

"Whoa tiger, what's going on there?" he asks in the dark, his hand staying exactly as it is.

"I don't know," I answer with honesty, blurting out things I shouldn't be blurting out. I blame the darkness and the silence. "To tell you the truth, I'm feeling a certain type of way. Is that weird?"

His thumb brushes the side of my hand. "I don't think so; it's very cozy in here."

Then, Davis laces his fingers through mine as if to punctuate the statement; it's big and warm and solid. Calloused, too. Somehow makes me feel safe and secure despite the fact that we are both in this bed because he was afraid. And not the other way around.

I'm definitely in the mood to snuggle.

Etcetera, etcetera.

Wonder what he would do if I roll to my side and put my hand on his broad chest. The thought makes me laugh because I know what he would do if I rolled over and put my hand on his chest: the man would accept the affection as any man would.

145

He's only human.

And he has a penis.

Plus, he is a loving guy.

I highly doubt he would shove me off of him even if he wanted to—Davis comes off as polite.

I have a feeling that he may be waiting to see what I'm going to do as we lay here—am I going to continue holding his hand, or am I going to make a different kind of move? *Where is this leading*, I can almost feel him wondering. *What is she going to do?*

Surely he doesn't think we're just going to lay here all night platonically holding hands? On the other hand—do I want to be the one to make the first move?

It seems to be a common theme in my relationships with the opposite sex.

"*There's nothing wrong with making the first move*," my mother's words go through my head. We've had this conversation a few times in the past after dating a string of men who were beta while I was on my quest to find me more of an alpha. "*What difference does it make who makes the first move*," she has preached more than once.

She's so wise.

Not sure what move I even want to make, I simply let us lay here staring up at the ceiling, wondering what time it is now that the minutes and hours are ticking by. Davis is going to be in rough shape tomorrow and I'm glad I get to sleep in even if he doesn't. I don't even want to know what time he has to be out the door.

One too many flights at dawn had me vowing never to book a flight before eight in the morning ever, ever again.

I won't lie, I'm getting a little squeamish with his thumb slowly caressing mine, which is totally ridiculous because it's just his thumb lightly rubbing on my skin—it's not like he's stroking my boobs or anything. It's basically the equivalent to a pat on the back for the most part; nothing sexual. Nothing to write home about.

So why is it giving me tingles down south?

Because you like him.

Really like him.

Ask him on a date then, for heaven's sake—don't put the moves on the dude while you're sharing a bed with him!

Um because I'd rather not wait?

God Juliet, you're worse than one of your students—those kids don't wait for jack squat and apparently you're no different.

Finally, rolling to my side to face him, I'm still holding his hand but letting my other hand rest on his bicep. He's wearing a tee shirt tonight and I'm able to touch his bare flesh, running my fingers up and down the crook of his arm.

I hear and feel him take a breath.

His skin is so soft...

"Juliet?"

"Hmm?" I hum, lost in the rhythm of drawing on his skin with the tip of my finger.

"Um, what are you doing?"

Not sure. "I'm not tired."

Davis lays quiet.

"Are you?" I ask to be polite because he hasn't said anything. It's making me nervous, making me second guess touching him like thism but if I pull back now, I'll only feel worse.

"No."

Up and down his thumb strokes over mine.

He's such a good guy and don't good guys deserve to be rewarded? Hot, sexy men who proved to be the opposite of everything you thought they would be?

Rewarded, Juliet? Are you HEARING yourself?

"Can I ask you something?"

My stomach flutters nervously. "Sure."

"What was your first impression of me?"

I stop moving my fingers along his arm, so I can concentrate on a reply. "My first impression of you? Well that is easy, I wanted you out of my face."

He shifts his body, taking his hand out from under mine and rolling my direction so our bodies are parallel, in the exact same position; feels around for my discarded hand and slides his palm back over it.

"I don't mean when you woke up and we were all standing over you—I meant afterwards." His low voice rumbles humorously.

"I don't think first impressions are easy to pinpoint because I had a million thoughts about you going through my head. You're a contradiction."

"What do you mean?"

"I mean—you don't look how you act?" Does that even make sense? "I'm not trying to sound like I stereotyped you, but I guess I based everything I knew about you on what I knew about Thad, which honestly isn't a lot."

"And you stereotyped him, too."

"It's hard not to, Davis. Put yourself in my position. A girl's best friend starts dating someone famous, who has fans and women chasing after him. So many stories about athletes cheating on their wives or girlfriends, having babies with their trainers or someone they met at a club." I move my shoulders up and down. "I was afraid for Mia—they dove right in, head first. It's been five months and I wouldn't be surprised if..."

I can't even say the words "get engaged" out loud.

I feel Davis nod. "It's not an easy life."

"Are you glad you're not a part of it anymore?"

"Most days. It's difficult watching a game without feeling a pang, you know? That's the part I miss. I was..." I hear him clearing a lump in his throat. "Good. I was really good."

Davis wasn't just really good—he was great. A star.

His football career was littered with accolades; I would know because I went down a rabbit hole of research the day Mia gave me his name in an attempt to woo me into coming on this trip.

Davis Halbrook was a running back at a Big Ten school in college, having been picked up early in the NFL Draft by the Chicago Steam before famously upsetting a heavily favored New England team at the Super Bowl to win the title.

Professionally he had a brief stint with a Miami team, the Oilers and another Super Bowl Championship-winning team before sustaining an injury that retired him at the age of thirty.

I squeeze the arm that has played for a national title, not realizing how exciting it could be sleeping next to a man with an insanely fit body.

Typically, I gravitate toward dad bods, but that's mostly due to my own insecurities.

Davis clears his throat again. "Do you like the outdoors?"

Mm. "I suppose? I grew up in a family that went to a cabin a lot in the summer. So, I like it and I'll do outdoorsy things, but I won't come up with the idea on my own."

He laughs, hand going to my hip. "What does that mean?"

"It means...if you wanted to go hiking, I'll go hiking. But I won't wake up in the morning and shoot out of bed and declare I want to go hiking, but I'll go." I pause. "I'm outdoorsy in a way, like, that I enjoy drinking on patios."

That makes him laugh, too, the front of our bodies almost pressed together, body heat warming me from the toes, knees, and other places I didn't know existed.

"I'm assuming you like it outside?"

"Sure," he says. "Snowboarding, snorkeling. I used to be into cave diving—I'd love to get back into that, it's been a long time."

Cave diving? Say again?

No.

"Would you go bungee jumping?" he asks.

"Hard no."

More laughing. "Why not?"

"Um because of death? Ropes snapping? Ropes getting tangled?"

"The statistics of that happening are like, a billion to one."

"False," I declare. "It's probably more like twelve percent of all bungee jumpers have their cord snap. No thanks."

"Uh—no, that's hot air balloons. That's far more deadly than bungee jumping."

I'm tempted to flip the light on so I can see if he's being serious or not. "Hot air balloons are not deadly."

"False!" he mimics me. "There is literally a balloon crash every single day. When I have my phone, I'll prove it. I bet you that right now, at this moment, someone in a hot air balloon is about to crash."

"You really are a worst-case scenario kind of guy, aren't you?"

"No. It's *facts.* I'm an optimist."

I roll my eyes and I'm certain he knows. "Blah blah blah, facts."

Davis seems to be mulling over another question. "What's your fondest memory of being at the cabin with your parents?"

That one I have to think about for a few seconds. "I'm not sure it's my fondest memory, but it's the one that sticks out the most. Back when I was a teenager, my parents had this speed boat, and I would have friends come to the lake with us and obviously we would go tubing behind the boat. Well, my father is nuts and his main goal was to flip us off the tube by driving like a maniac."

Davis chuckles as I tell my story.

"So I have my friend Claire along, right? And we're on this

tube called Big Bertha—and I can see that my father is barely paying attention as he's driving this boat because he keeps turning his head around to look at us. Mom is in the boat spotting, but so was Dad even though he's not supposed to be. Anyway, Big Bertha hits a pocket of air and a wave and Claire and I go flying into the air—she's able to hang on but I go sailing into the water and my swimsuit gets jammed up my ass." I'm shocked I didn't get a concussion. "I shit you not, I was walking crooked for an entire week—and I've not been tubing since."

Davis is quiet a few seconds. "Dang, I'm glad we didn't take the speed boat out this weekend. Don't want you reliving any childhood trauma."

"Ha ha, thanks, I appreciate it." He's not wrong; it was traumatic! "What's your fondest childhood memory?"

"I'm not sure. We didn't have a lot of money and my mom was gone a lot, so...I guess my fondest memories were...hmm. It was a huge splurge to get ice cream. A *huge* splurge. I always got bubble gum and a scoop of blue moon."

I nod approvingly. "Classic childhood flavors. I went with ice cream that had chocolate, if we got ice cream." My parents did well for themselves, but Dad really wasn't into spending money on meals, dining out, or tasty treats. Every so often, Mom could convince him to stop at a roadside ice cream shop along the highway on our way to the cabin in the summers, but he'd grumble and groan about it the entire time.

And he never got himself ice cream.

It's no wonder that Davis helps support his sister if she's a single mother—he was raised by one.

"I used to talk Penelope into doing the dumbest shit when we were young; my mom was always at work so we were left alone a lot—she couldn't afford babysitters. So we'd ride cardboard boxes down the basement stairs and have sword fights with butter knives and once we had a yard sale while Mom was gone. Holy shit we got in so much trouble when I sold the lawn mower to some dude for ten bucks."

"Ten bucks!" I gasp. "The guy should have known better buying it from a kid!"

"No doubt." He sounds amused. "I'd question it if some kid was hocking a lawn mower on the side of the road, that's for damn sure."

"I'd at least give him fifty for it," I tease. "Then I'd be able to sleep at night."

"Fifty!" Davis cackles. "You'd still be stealing it!"

"I know, I'm kidding."

His hand is on my hip, beginning a slow caress. "You're funny."

His voice is low and gravelly.

I swallow. "You think so?"

"I know so." Up and down my hip that hand goes, singeing holes into my flesh through my jogging pants that have never once been jogging.

His voice is so terribly sexy.

My limbs go weak.

Still, I move closer, laying my head on the arm I have extended, fingertips brushing the headboard.

Prime position for a smooch on the lips.

"Juliet?" He says my name for the second time in the dark.

"Yes?"

"So, don't judge me for asking this, but I'm a little confused and just need some clarification so I'm not jumping to conclusions..."

Oh boy.

"Okay..." My tone comes out as hesitant as his. I cannot imagine what he's about to ask.

"Were you...*are* you...trying to..."

Oh shit.

He's going to say it. *He's going to ask if I want to kiss him.*

He's calling me out.

I freeze like a statue, though his hand is still on my hip.

Deny it.

Deny, deny, deny.

"Are you trying to..." Davis is having the damnedest time getting the words out, his shyness tugging at my heartstrings. Gosh he's so cute.

"Kiss me?"

"Am I trying to kiss *you*?" I repeat his question for lack of anything more brilliant to say: if I say yes, he might laugh. If I say no, he may not move in closer.

I feel like a teenager.

It feels like a wonderful place to be; somewhere I haven't been in a very long time—enamored with a man.

Impressed by a man.

I'm going to miss him.

"Yes. Is that what this is?"

Erm.

Yes?

"Do you think it's possible I want to kiss a man that only has one eyebrow? I swear to God, I can still smell the char and frying hair."

Now why the hell would I go and say an insensitive, stupid thing like that?

Ugh, I'm such an idiot.

"You cannot smell the char," Davis laughs in the dark.

"You're right, I'm just saying that to tease you. But for real, I don't think I'm sexually attracted to men with one eyebrow."

Even as I say this, I put my hand on his waist, letting it settle into the curve. Move my thumb back and forth near the hem of his tee shirt.

"When have you ever met another man with only one eyebrow?"

I shrug. "Men? None. Women? A few. My mother went through a phase of severely over plucking her brows, which practically rendered them bare. My youth was an age of very thin eyebrows and frosted lipstick."

That makes Davis chuckle. "It's going to grow back, I swear."

"But you only have that one brow now."

"Are you discriminating?" He pauses to ask, "Wait, do I still only have one brow if it's too dark and you can't see my face at all?"

This is an excellent point; a very astute, valid point!

"Hmm, that's a good question." My fingers toy with the edge of his cotton shirt, flirting with the skin beneath.

"I'm very smart, didn't you know that? I should have been a lawyer." We both laugh softly at that. "Is this entire conversation about my eyebrows a stall tactic, or do you legitimately not want to kiss me? I was being serious when I asked."

Moment of truth. Time to fess up.

Putting on my big girl panties and asking for what I want, Juliet.

Instead I say, "Truth or Dare."

Him: "Truth."

"Were you thinking about kissing me?"

"That one is easy—of course I was, yes."

"So why didn't you?"

Davis scoffs. "It's not your turn to ask another question."

"Ugh—you're infuriating."

"Am I?" His hands go back and forth along my side, hand curving over my backside.

"No."

"Truth or dare."

This is an easy one. "Truth."

"Were you thinking of kissing me?"

Duh. "Yes."

Silence fills the cabin of the camper, our breathing and breath mingle with the sound of the wind.

"Alright."

Um. Alright what?

He wants to kiss me, I want to kiss him, so why isn't he embracing me or whatever dudes do when they're putting the first moves on a lady?

Do I still have to make the first move, is that what he's doing over there? Waiting?

I clear my throat.

"So..." my voice trails off in the dark as his hands trail along my rear.

"So..." he lets his voice trail off, too.

Could this be any more awkward?

He still smells fresh, though it's late; like mint toothpaste and aftershave lotion but also campfire and the woods, the combination causing my mouth to water.

We're lying facing one another on the bed, both of us on our sides, both of us with one hand on each other. I'm not quite sure what to do with mine—I don't want to slide it anywhere and have it land where I don't want it or where it's inappropriate considering our lips haven't even touched. On the other hand, I wouldn't mind if his hand slid up my shirt; he's been toying with the hem of it this entire time while he's been caressing my butt.

He is being so polite. I think that's where my hang up is; I'm used to men who go at it hard, who don't mind having sex on the first date, who could care less what my last name is, where I'm from, what my hobbies are—things like that.

This whole chivalry thing feels slightly foreign.

I clear my throat again.

Davis clears his.

"Would you knock it off," I laugh.

"You knock it off," he echoes, being a flirt.

"Why aren't you doing anything?" I finally blurt out—it's easier when he's not able to see my face or the blush taking over my cheeks. My face is on fire.

"It's more fun this way."

"Really it's not."

"And why is that?"

Because of the sexual tension I now have on the brain, and the tingling of my spine. The flutters in my stomach. The urge I have right now to shiver even though it's not cold.

None of this is fun; all of it is embarrassing.

"Why is this not fun?" I have to ask because I need more explanation. If I was a man, there would be blood rushing from my brain to places I only need for screwing. But I don't have a penis and can only speak to the wetness growing between my thighs.

Not. Fun. And now he wants me to explain?

Hardly.

"Yeah, what's not fun about this? I'm having a great time." He shifts on the bed, his big body making a dent in the flimsy mattress, causing me to roll forward a bit simply from the motion.

Men are so different than women.

Here I am overthinking everything while he lays there having jolly good fun at my expense.

My bottom lip juts out stubbornly; I want a kiss, dammit, and he's making me work for it!

"You know, I can hear you thinking over there." His hand gives my rear a playful pat, gliding up my back and over my spine, over my shirt but still causing those ripples of pleasure to course through my lower half.

The daintiest of snorts escape my nose. "Oh you can, hey? What am I thinking about since you're so darn smart?"

"You're wondering why we're just laying here after we both just admitted we want to kiss each other."

He sounds so pleased with himself, but also, he is one hundred thousand percent correct.

Davis follows it up with an, "Is that true?"

I shrug as a reply and he laughs. "You're stubborn, aren't you?"

"I can be." I find myself easing into the laughter, the tension that is barely there, how easy it is to talk to him. So comfortable as if we've known each other for years…

My body relaxes and I snuggle closer, allowing myself to give in, burrowing into his front like a hedgehog seeking warmth. Davis wraps his arms around me, hands sliding up and down my arms. Across my back. Up the back of my neck and into my hair.

That's more like it…

If you're not going to kiss me, at least give me a scalp massage.

Between us, I feel the stirring of a hardening erection and smirk into his firm chest, lips curling with a knowing smile as my tits press against him.

I wiggle.

"You're doing that on purpose, aren't you?" He chuckles above me, chin resting at the top of my skull.

Does he know nothing about women and how we operate?

"Probably."

Never have I ever met a guy so contrary to what I thought he would be. He certainly does not come off as the kind of guy who is a bit shy or reserved; one would think that Davis Halbrook was commanding and dominant—seems I'm the one that's both of those things.

Casually—as casually and cool as I can muster—I move my hand from his arm and let it drag slowly to the center of his chest, skimming along his back muscles. He's solid as a rock, and warm. Laying still he lets me explore, his breath hitching when I brush over his nipple. We're not going to fool around or get naked, but I do want his mouth on mine...just to see.

I have to see what it's like.

Not only because it's been so many months since I've been kissed, but because...well.

It's him.

While I'm overthinking everything, I feel Davis's warm, minty breath mingling with mine—a sure sign he's coming in for the kill. Instinctively my lips part.

My heart races a million beats per second and I thank God above that we're laying down on the bed because I swear my limbs have gone weak; arms and legs and hands are jelly and completely useless.

I wouldn't be able to walk if I had to.

Our mouths connect, lips touching softly.

Shocks of electricity.

Magic.

His lips are perfect; full and undemanding. Soft.

Whatever noises were outside—whatever thing or people —fade away until it's just us here snuggling, kissing and enjoying the moment.

For a while we only press our lips together; there is no tongue or saliva involved.

I kiss the corner of his mouth; he kisses the corner of mine.

Then my chin.

Then the tip of my nose.

I kiss the spot next to his eye after locating it gently with my fingers—it's my favorite spot, tender and soft.

Our mouths meet again, this time braver, getting along splendidly.

More confident.

Davis is the first one of us to part his mouth, inviting our tongues to co-mingle and I take the opportunity almost bashfully. Timidly exploring, not wanting to stick the whole thing in his mouth.

Gross, I'm not that kind of girl.

Er.

Only sometimes and this is not one of those times.

Davis's mouth is like a dream, his tongue minty and sweet, both at the same time. Not demanding—but he's also taking the lead, hand still at the back of my nape, fingers still plunged into my hair.

"You taste good."

He moans.

I moan.

It's one of those kinds of kisses.

The kind that curls your toes and makes you want to dry hump like two teenagers sneaking around in your parents' basement. The kind of kiss that has a man's hand easing into your sweatshirt and gliding up your stomach and you don't even care that it's not flat or that you ate a dozen marshmallows the night before.

The kiss is that good.

His large palm covers my boob, thumb brushing over my nipple.

I have no idea how we are going to sleep after this, but *we only discussed kissing and it's only kissing we will do.* I may be horny and hard-up but I have the willpower of a saint.

Or a nun.

Pity that.

"You feel so good," he tells me as his palm cups my breast, caressing it until my breath hitches. It hitches again when he abandons it to head south, hand sliding down my stomach and over my belly button. Teases the hem of my sleep bottoms; leaves my heart racing.

"This was such a terrible idea," he tells me. "How can we be expected to stop?

How can this be a terrible idea when his hands feel so good down my pants? How can this be a terrible idea when his index fingers begins a unhurried, but steady circle over my clit?

It feels too good to be terrible.

His mouth. His hands. The heat from his body keeping me warm.

"We should have just kept our hands to ourselves." I declare with zero conviction, running a hand through his hair. "Then this wouldn't be an issue."

I nod solemnly, eyes almost rolling to the back of my head as his fingers work their magic. "And now we have to live with ourselves."

It's then that I realize I don't want him to be gone when I wake up in the morning. I want to open my eyes, look over to his side and see him beside me.

I don't want him to go.

———

DAVIS IS GONE IN THE MORNING WHEN I RISE.

I roll over as the sun pours through the camper's small windows, I squint, aware of the fact the bed is cold and the sheets are pushed back and wrinkled, evidence that a man had been sleeping there the night before.

We'd fooled around before falling asleep, the memory bringing a small, tired smile to my mouth—*the mouth he'd kissed until I needed Chapstick.*

With anyone else I may be offended that he just slipped out of bed and snuck off, but I know he had an early flight: seven o'clock to be exact. I'd asked Thad.

Over an hour drive to the airport, checking bags and needing to arrive early, Davis had awoken around four, if I had to guess.

So no—I am not blaming him for stealing away without a good-bye.

I ease out of bed, tired as hell, needing another five good hours of sleep. Ha!

First things first: pee and brush my teeth, breakfast for sure, all in that order.

There on the mirror of the bathroom, in bold masculine scrawl, is a note:

JULIET,

SORRY I MISSED YOU THIS MORNING. HAD TO BE OUT THE DOOR FOR AN EARLY FLIGHT.

THANKS FOR THE LATE NIGHT SNUGGLES.

P.S.: DID YOU KNOW YOU DROOL IN YOUR SLEEP?

SO CUTE.

XOXO DAVIS

Cute?

Cute?!

Do I know I drool in my sleep?

Do I?

Oh god.

My fingers fly to my lips, pressing on the corners of my mouth. How could he possibly know I drool in my sleep? It was dark in the room and I wasn't...

Oh.

He's messing with me.

Briefly as I brush my teeth, I wonder where the paper came from, and the tape. I'm also grateful he's not here because I look terrible.

Sleep deprived.

Bedraggled.

A hot mess.

Mia confirms this when she nudges me at the little buffet tables, a simple self-serve breakfast.

"Girl, you look tired. How late were you up?"

She should talk; Mia has bedhead and bags under her eyes, signs that she was up as late as I was, probably making sexy sex with her boyfriend at the same time I was making out with his best friend.

"Late enough," I grin to myself, spooning scrambled eggs onto my plate.

She does the same, side-eyeing me. "What's this look about?"

"What look?"

"You look..." She stops and cocks her head. "Wait, turn and look at me."

I turn and look at her. "What?"

Her eyes scan my face, stopping at my mouth. "Are those..."

I shift under her scrutiny. "Are those what?"

"Your lips look puffy."

I grin again. "Do they? Weird."

"Juliet Jocelyn Robertson! Were you making out with Davis last night?"

Who else could it have been? And how in the hell did she guess that merely because my lips are puffy? Maybe I was sucking on a lemon this morning for all she knows.

I shrug, non-committed. "Maybe?"

Mia gasps. "Oh my god—I knew it."

"Knew what?"

"I knew you'd hit it off." She fist pumps more than once, and as she's about to do it a third time, I stop her.

"Please don't. This isn't Jersey Shore."

Her arm goes down to her side. "Sorry." She sidles up next to me, bumping our hips together, but lowering her voice. "I knew you'd hit it off." Mia sighs. "It's too bad he had to leave so early."

I nod. "It's too bad we all have to leave. Another day would have been fun."

Fun. Enlightening.

Sexy, perhaps?

What would have happened with Davis if we'd all stayed one more day?

Distracted, my best friend begins plucking fruit from the serving platter and placing it onto her plate one by one, inspecting each and every strawberry.

"So, um, about that."

I keep putting food on my plate, and dare I say, I detect a little reluctance in her tone?

"Just say it," I tell her, knowing she has something to share.

Mia intakes a breath. "Thad and I are going to stay."

"What do you mean you're going to stay?" I glance over at her. "What for?"

"He wants to do more on the water. He thought three days would be enough, but clearly, he wants to play. We'll be home in a few more days."

I suppose it's not the end of the world that I have to make for the airport myself.

"Too bad Davis left so early; you could have driven with him."

Possibly made out in the van...

"There is no way in hell I'd want to be up as early as he was." I shudder to illustrate my point, stealing one of her berries and popping it on my tongue. "Too bad, who knows when I'll see him again."

CHAPTER 9

Davis

"...**I**s Uncle Davis dead?"

"...*No, baby girl—he's definitely alive. See his chest moving up and down?*"

"...*Maybe we should check just to be sure. We can hold a mirror under his big nose. If it fogs up, we'll know.*"

"...*That's very smart of you, how did you know that?*"

"*I saw it on an episode of Lost.*"

"*You shouldn't be watching that; it's for grownups.*"

There's a pause. "*Okay, but can we still check Uncle Davis's vitals?*"

"*Skip, I could hear him snoring before we even walked in the door.*"

Snoring?

What? Who's snoring?

I wipe at the corner of my mouth and feel moisture.

"Gross," my niece says. "Is that drool?"

"I'm too cool to drool."

I stay flat on my back, arm slung over my eyes to block out the light.

"Oh yeah, he's definitely alive." I feel Penelope give my feet a nudge with her knee at the foot of my bed.

"Who let you scoundrels in here?"

"We did. There's a car outside and a woman at your door and Skipper wanted to investigate."

"What time is it?" I roll to my side. "How long have I been asleep?"

I've been home a week now and hit the ground running after that short trip with Mia, Thad, and Juliet; left town again for a meeting in Texas almost as soon as I returned.

Just needed a respite from my stressful day; a short nap. However, from the looks of it, I passed out a few hours longer than I'd intended.

It's damn near dark outside.

"What time is it?" My sister chuckles at my question.

"Dinner time. We just got home and were going to invite you over, I grabbed a pizza."

Skipper pokes me in the arm impatiently. "But that lady is downstairs."

Oh right.

The lady downstairs.

"What do you mean by *down*stairs."

"The kitchen. She brought you something."

A lady is in my kitchen and brought me something? That makes no sense.

"What lady?"

My niece bounces on her heels. "Juliet."

Juliet? I throw back the blanket I'd covered up with and sit up. "Juliet is here?"

"Whoa, someone is in a rush." Penelope laughs, stepping out of the way to make more room in my crowded bedroom. Her hand circles the top of her own head. "Maybe fix that."

It takes me a few moments before I realize my sister and

niece are still standing there watching me hustle around my room, smoothing down my hair and straightening my clothes.

"Could one or both of you please go downstairs, so that Juliet's not down there by herself?" She probably hears us up here. Lord only knows what she thinks could be going on.

"Maybe she wants to stay and eat with us?" my niece says hopefully—she loves meeting new people.

Sweet as pie, that little nugget.

"Oh shit, you're right." My sister springs into action, grabbing Skipper by the hand and leading her toward the door. "Come on, let's go entertain Uncle Davis's guest."

She says it in a way only a sister would; full of suspicion and unanswered questions.

I can't for the life of me imagine why Juliet would be at my house. Ordinarily I would also wonder where she got my information or my address, but I already know the answer to that: Thad.

And, why didn't she call or text before popping in unannounced?

Seems out of character for her, but then again, I don't know her all that well.

I pull the tee shirt over my head that I'd just slept in and pull on a clean half zip fleece, give myself a once-over in the bathroom mirror, and bound down the stairs.

"...you my uncle's new girlfriend?"

"Skipper, don't be rude," my sister admonishes my niece.

Juliet takes the question in stride. "Um, no, sweetie, he and I met on a trip with his best friend Thad. Do you know Thad?"

"Yeah, Uncle Thad always brings me a Barbie when he visits." Skipper takes a deep breath. "Do you like dogs, do you like cats, what's your favorite color? Do you like ice cream?"

I catch Juliet's soft, "Whoa nelly, that's a lot of questions all at once!" before strolling through the kitchen door.

I stop short, pretending I hadn't known anyone was in the kitchen, damned if I didn't.

"Hey! Juliet—oh hey! What...how are you?" I move in for the cursory, noncommittal hug. Taking a whiff of her before pulling away, stupid smile plastered to my face. "What brings you here?"

"I am so sorry." Her eyes dart around the room—at my sister, at my niece, both avidly watching with wide eyed stares, not even bothering to hide their interest. "I wasn't sure how to get ahold of you, so I just asked Thad for your address."

It's not shocking that my family is gawking at her, considering they're both incredibly nosy, always in my business, and haven't seen a woman in my house since Willa moved out.

In and out in less than two months.

Cringe.

"You couldn't get ahold of me?" In this day and age? It doesn't take a rocket scientist to look a person up on the internet and have access to their information at the click of a button.

Facebook. The Gram. LinkedIn.

The Tok.

The emails.

"I tried calling and texting, but the number wasn't working?"

"Which number were you using?" I'm curious.

She holds the phone out and I glance at it. "That's not my number. It's nine nine four, not nine nine three."

"Well that makes sense then—I thought for a second you'd blocked me."

"I can't block you if I don't have your number."

I catch my sister's gaze over the top of Juliet's head. *Really?* It's saying. *What the hell kind of weird flirting is this?*

Juliet thrusts something toward me—something I recognize that's most definitely mine.

My tablet.

"I'd wondered where that had gone!" I take it from her. "I messaged the campground, but Ben hadn't seen it."

"I found it while I was packing my things. Figured I'd see you soon enough but..."

Clearing my throat, I shift the focus.

Try to catch my sister's eye and send her a nonverbal message: leave.

Get out.

Take Skipper and GO.

Penelope ignores me, easing onto the barstool at the kitchen counter and pulling a green grape out of the bowl on the counter, popping it in her mouth.

"So you met on the camping trip?"

"Yes," Juliet fills her in on the details. "I'm Mia's best friend. Thad and she thought it would be a good idea to stick your brother and me in the same camper."

"Ooh, love that," Penelope hums, not helpful at all. "How did you get along?"

"Great," I tell her abruptly. "Isn't your pizza getting cold? Skipper must be hungry."

"Nope—I'll warm it up." Penelope happily remains rooted to the spot, digging for information. "Had the two of you met before?"

"No—that was our first time."

Penelope nods along. "What was your first impression of my brother?"

"Did you think he was handsomeeee?" Skipper intones, in on her mother's schtick.

"Good question, Skip." My sister high-fives her seven-year-old daughter.

They are totally in cahoots.

"Did you kiss?" Skipper adds, betraying me on so many levels.

1. She's embarrassing me in front of a pretty woman.
2. She's definitely embarrassing Juliet, whose face has turned crimson red.
3. These questions are way too personal.
4. Actually, I'd definitely answer that last one if Juliet wasn't standing in the room because: why not. We did, in fact, kiss.

Regardless, Penelope needs to teach Skipper how to use a filter; they look way too pleased with themselves.

Two peas in a pod on a mission to get me married.

"What do you do, Juliet?" my sister asks her because she just can't help herself.

"I'm a teacher—middle school, actually. It's pretty much the worst age ever," she laughs good-humoredly while my sister nods her head in agreement.

"I was a camp counselor when I was in college for middle schoolers, and I remember a group of girls who kept trying to sneak out of their two-story windows because it was on a college campus and they were rooming in the dorms. Can you believe that? Sneaking out of a two-story window? Who does that?"

"Those of us who think we're invincible? Usually you're around the age of twelve when it starts?" My sister and Juliet laugh.

I butt in, seeing no choice.

I have to put an end to this little tea party love fest. I don't want my sister getting too cozy with someone she's probably never going to see again. Skipper, either—I wouldn't intentionally bring anyone around unless I thought they were going to stay around. Not after that whole debacle with Willa. Skipper took it harder than I did for sure.

Those little seven-year-old hearts get broken pretty easily

—her dad's not in the picture, so I'm the only father figure she's ever had.

"Okay, you two, let me quickly chat with Juliet and I'll be over for dinner."

"She should come for pizza," Skipper announces. "Juliet, do you want to come?"

Juliet shakes her head. "No, sweetie, but thank you for the invitation. I just needed to drop your uncle's tablet off—seems we don't live that far from one another after all." She's smiling at me and my gaze goes to her lips.

That mouth.

I remember it well.

Sweet and soft and delicious.

Like her boobs.

Fuck, I need to get my sister out of my house. Love them to death, but they gots to go.

Is there nothing I can do to get my sister to leave? She's obviously getting the hint; she's just not taking it, enjoying this way too much. If Penelope and Skipper want to get me married off so badly, perhaps they should give me privacy instead of meddling and wanting to watch me make a muddle of things on my own.

I don't actually need their help—I tend to do just fine with the ladies on my own, but for some reason these two feel the need to facilitate my romantic situations. For example, any time we go to the grocery store as a trio, my sister will make a show of using the word *brother* instead of my name, or practically shouting the word niece at full volume if there is a woman nearby.

"*Women love babies and puppies,*" she has told me in the past. "*It's like chick magnets. Work with what God gave you— an adorable niece.*"

Yeah, yeah.

How about she takes some of her *own* advice, considering

she's single and claims she's ready to mingle. Penelope hasn't been on a date in...well, it's been longer for her than it has been for me.

What a fine pair we make.

I take care of her and she takes care of me, but right now, I want to talk to Juliet alone.

Reluctantly—ever so reluctantly—the girls finally leave, Penelope watching me over her shoulder as she exits the room, practically needing to shove my niece along to get her out.

Little scamp.

"So *that* was my sister..." Not that I need to give her an explanation—they're the ones that found Juliet outside the house and let her in.

"She looks just like you."

"Does she?"

"Practically twins."

"Except for the height and the voice."

Juliet concurs. "Same hair, same smile, same twinkle in your eyes."

"I have a twinkle in my eye?" That's news to me; at least, no one has ever told me that. "That's fun."

"A twinkle in your eye is fun?"

"Sure. It's very...Santa like."

Juliet laughs. "Dear lord, don't compare yourself to Santa."

"Why not?"

Her lips press together; instantly I know she's thinking something naughty.

"Say it."

Juliet shakes her head.

"Come on, say it."

Hesitantly, she sighs and leans her body against my countertop. "No one wants to *bang* Santa Claus."

Bang.

Screw.

"I'd say come again so you repeat that, but it would just sound pervy considering we both know I heard you the first time."

Juliet rolls her eyes, amusement dancing there.

Good, I'm glad she's entertained, beats her being offended by my off-color comment. Yeah, I can be immature sometimes, but what dude isn't?

I go around the counter to the sink, nervous to have her in my space and in my home—seeing her out of place, i.e., not in the woods—seems surreal. Different.

For starters she's wearing a dress. She must have worn it to work today because it's a little more playful than serious, with hearts on the skirt and bright pink top. She's tied a sash around her waist and on her feet? Pink high heeled shoes. Juliet's hair is done up in a sleek ponytail and she has on large gold hoop earrings. Totally gorgeous.

Jeez, half the pre-teenage boys in her classes must have huge crushes on her—I know I would have.

The past few nights I've had a dream or two about the hot little teacher. Sure, one of two of them may have included bears, but waking up with a raging boner with Juliet's face on the brain isn't the worst way to wake up.

"I see that your eyebrow is growing back in."

I reach up to touch it with a smirk on my face. "Yeah—not to brag, but I have hair there now."

Not a ton of it, but at least I'm not lopsided anymore and my hair is dark, so it's obvious that new growth is happening. Basically my brow has five o'clock shadow...

"You don't have to enter rooms backwards anymore," she teases.

"I've had to enter a few rooms this week, and let me tell you, having to retell the story over and over was like swallowing humble pie." There's nothing worse than explaining to grown men—professional athletes, both men and women, all of whom say whatever is on their mind—how in the hell my eyebrow was burnt to a crisp.

"Wait wait wait—tell me that one more time," Darnell Pruit had begged during the meeting we were having about his retirement and investments.

"Darnell, I didn't fly all this way to talk about my eyebrow."

He was fixated on it.

"I burnt one of mine off once, but I was fourteen and it was at a house party. Not squatting around a damn campfire, man." He'd whooped and hollered at my story, essentially calling me a pussy, though not in those exact terms.

"Can we move on?" I'd shuffled and reshuffled the papers.

Darnell's eyes could not stay focused, instead lingering on my forehead. "I'm sorry, bro, but I can't. Can I take a selfie with you?"

And on it had gone, all week, through most of my meetings.

What a waste of time, travel, and money.

Should have cancelled and rescheduled until I had hair growing in.

What an idiotic problem to have.

"Well the good news is, you're almost back to normal," Juliet quips, still perched on a barstool.

"Normal? I wouldn't call me normal, but...okay, if you insist."

"Oh please," she scoffs. "You're about as normal as it comes. Name one way you're not. Just one."

Hmm.

I brace my hands on the cold, stone counter and lean forward so I can think.

And think.

And think.

Okay this is harder than I thought, I guess I am pretty normal? No fetishes, no criminal convictions, never broken the law. Don't drink much or smoke. Never smoked pot.

Go to bed and wake up early.

Goddamn I'm boring.

"Well?" Juliet nudges me.

"Fine. You're right, I guess I am pretty normal."

Juliet tilts her head. "Why are you saying that like it's a bad thing? Do you know how hard it is to find a guy who isn't a complete douche?"

I raise my chin up. "Who says I'm not a complete douche?"

Just once I'd like to be called an asshole or a dickhead, it seems like such a badass thing to be called.

"Are you serious? Davis, I spent the weekend with you. You're not sarcastic, you're polite, you were nice to Cookie and Erik even though they kept giving you 'the eyes.' You held my hair back and tucked me in—which you did not have to do. You were respectful and a gentleman and didn't so much as touch me inappropriately, not once."

She sounds a little disgruntled as she delivers that last part. "Is that a bad thing?"

Juliet shrugs and studies her fingernails. "No." Long pause. "Not necessarily."

That has me laughing. "You're hard to figure out, Juliet...Juliet..." I fumble for a last name, realizing I have no idea what hers is.

"Robertson," she supplies. "Juliet Jocelyn Robertson."

If that isn't one of the prettiest names I've ever heard...

We begin a staring contest then, neither of us saying anything more, her full name lingering in the space between us. It's dark outside now and the house is quiet as a tomb; intimate. Only the glow from some flameless candles illuminates the space since I haven't flicked any lights on yet.

Our showdown is interrupted by the ringing of my phone; it's still on vibrate from my nap and quivers on the countertop, buzzing and buzzing and scaring the shit out of Juliet and I.

"It's Thad," I tell her. "He's video chatting me."

She nods. "Go ahead and answer it—see what he wants."

Thad and Mia should be well on their way home by now, having spent those extra few days doing whatever it was they were doing in the middle of the woods.

I hit the green button to take the call, coming around to Juliet's side of the counter so we can all chat. It would be rude to exclude her and pretend she wasn't in the room.

"Hey, buddy—what's going on?" I shift the phone, so she and I are both in the frame. "Juliet is here."

Thad waves and Mia's face pops into the camera.

"Good!" Mia claps. "We tried calling and calling you ,but you didn't answer!"

Juliet sticks her face in my phone. "I was here! I'm dropping off Davis's tablet—I didn't know if he needed it or not. We're just sitting here talking."

"Talking?" Thad deadpans. "Why is it so damn dark?"

I move toward the outlet, flipping on the lights above the island. "Happy now?"

"Yes, we want to be able to see your faces," Thad says.

"We have something to tell you and we wanted to do it together."

Oh boy.

Ohhhh boy.

I know where this is going.

I glance over at Juliet to see if she's coming to the same conclusion, but judging by her neutral expression, she hasn't figured it out yet.

"We're engaged!" Thad and Mia shout at the same time,

thrusting Mia's hand into the camera, a giant, sparkling rock twinkling and winking back at us.

"Holy shit!" Juliet blurts out. "Oh my god!" She hesitates, lightbulb going off. "Oh my god, is that the reason you stayed behind and didn't come home?"

Thad nods. "Yeah, this seemed like the perfect place to pop the question. We rowed out in a boat this afternoon—"

"—He brought a picnic."

"—And I proposed in the middle of the lake."

"It was perfect!" Mia preens, extending her hand out of view but so obviously admiring her new, shiny ring. "I was shocked!"

"Mia, I am so happy for you!" Juliet is clutching her hands to her chest, like someone would do when they were looking at a cute puppy, or basking in love, and looks genuinely happy for her best friend—not that I thought she wouldn't be.

"So now what's the plan?"

"I don't know, we've been talking about it a little bit—we've only been engaged for an hour—but I don't think we want a long engagement. We'll see."

This is what they call a whirlwind romance.

Quick courtship. Early engagement. Wedding soon to follow.

Happens sometimes with professional athletes, they want to balance their playing time with their free time, which isn't an easy juggling act.

Mia and Thad both prattle on, talking over one another in their excitement, kissing and flirting all the while they're video chatting with Juliet and I.

I have to admit, it's making me a tad envious, a feeling I rarely feel.

Beside me, Juliet lets out a wistful sigh and I figure she must be feeling the same way. A little envious, a little longing.

Without overthinking it, I put my arm around her shoulders and squeeze, accidentally kissing the crown of her head.

If Mia and Thad notice, they don't spare it a comment.

If Juliet thinks anything of it, she doesn't say a word.

For another ten minutes, our best friends go on about how happy they are and retell the proposal story several more times.

"We have to call my parents back," Thad says. "They were at dinner with friends when we called before."

Juliet and I nod.

"We love you guys!" Mia squeals. "Oh my god, I just can't believe it!" She's beaming. "We should go."

After another few minutes of saying good-bye, the call disconnects and Juliet and I are left in the same place we were before the video chat: in complete silence.

In the air is a different kind of vibe.

One of...shock. A weird combination of happy and confusion. No, that's not the right word for it. I am happy, it's just... I don't know how to feel or what this is.

You are not losing your best friend, you are gaining a new friend: Mia. You already only see him every so often, it's not like you were up each other's asses—she is not stealing your best friend.

I clear my throat.

"What are you thinking right now?" Juliet asks slowly. "I can't tell what's going on in your brain right now."

"I'm..." I don't know.

She nods knowingly. "Yeah, me too."

"I am...speechless?" *If a person can be speechless when they have words coming out of their mouth.* "I'm stunned. He did it —he actually did it."

"That's an understatement if I've ever heard one," Juliet mumbles sliding off the barstool, moving around the counter to the sink. She goes to the cabinet and pulls out a glass, filling it with water and chugging it. "I wish this was stronger."

"We're happy for them," I say.

"We are!" Her tone is a bit too cheerful. "We are so happy for them!"

"This is what they wanted."

Juliet nods, chugging more water. "They are such good people, they one hundred percent deserve to be happy."

So are we.

So do we.

After Juliet sets down the water glass, she glances up at me. "Did you know he was proposing this weekend?"

"Not really." I think back to previous conversations and come up blank on anything remotely related to a proposal this weekend. Sure, he's mentioned it but nothing concrete.

"Really? He never said anything to you? It surprises me that he wouldn't have hit you up for some advice before popping the question..."

"I mean, I knew he was *thinking* about it—we talk about everything—I just wasn't sure he was going to do it this past weekend. Guess he couldn't wait—the ring must have been burning a hole in his pocket."

"Had he showed it to you beforehand?"

Yes, actually, he had shown me a few rings beforehand. A few that they'd found together while playfully scrolling through Instagram that Mia thought were pretty; she hadn't wanted to choose her own ring, wanted it to be a surprise. Still he'd had an inkling as to what style she liked, and had shown me.

We'd joked about it, but as far as I knew, the proposal was farther off in the future.

"Just a picture of it when he was at the jewelry store—and this was a few weeks ago, and he got busy with work. Tons of traveling, you know? It's the start of the season so he's laser focused."

I used to be the same way. Willa might have been a shitty human and a shitty girlfriend, but she understood the lifestyle and as far as that part went—she was perfect.

These days, I don't have to worry about working, practice and traveling—not the same kind of working and traveling. Less stress and no impact on my physical or mental health. Makes sense that Thad would want to move things along...

Here one day, gone the next.

Careers, women, *the life*.

CHAPTER 10
Juliet

Mia and Thad are engaged.

I can hardly wrap my brain around it.

I mean I can...

...but I can't.

Mia is getting married.

Married!!!

Just this past weekend we were on a trip together. Just two weeks before that, we were sharing drinks together as she convinced me to go on said trip together.

And here we are...

I'm sitting in a man's kitchen I slept with.

Fine, not technically, but it was intimate just the same— the same way sitting in his dimly lit kitchen feels.

When I'd gotten to his house, I'd stood on the stoop knocking—not wanting to ring the doorbell and be annoying after the first time I'd rung it and no one had come to the door. But his truck was in the driveway and I'd assumed he was inside?

"Are you looking for my Uncle Davis?"

A little girl had appeared out of nowhere, through the

hedgerow, and came bouncing up to me with a coat and rain boots on.

Skipper.

That's the only person this could possibly be.

"I am looking for Uncle Davis." That sounded weird. I tried again. "Mister Halbrook."

Skipper laughed. "That sounds funny, no one calls him that."

"Yeah, that did sound funny." I glanced up at the façade of the house—it was a beautiful red brick colonial, larger than I would have imagined and ten times classier.

A very adult-like house.

Expensive.

I was taken aback when I'd entered the subdivision and even more astonished when I'd matched the address on the mailbox to the one I had written on a sheet of paper.

"Do I have the right house?" I asked the tiny girl with brown hair and big brown eyes. Her hair fell in two, tidy braids, tied at the bottom with bubble gum pink bows.

"Yup, this is where he lives." She eyeballed the tablet in my hand. "Are you selling Girl Scout Cookies?"

"Er, no, I'm here to drop this off."

She came closer to inspect the electronic in its black, leather case. "Did you find it?"

"Yes, he left it behind somewhere." There was no way I was telling this impressionable child he and I were sharing a room together and he forgot it because he was stumbling around, packing in the dark.

"Oh." Skipper inhaled to say something new. "We have pizza if you want some."

Had this child never heard of stranger danger? She couldn't just be inviting random people off the street to eat with her, dear lord, where was her mother?

"I really just need to drop this off and I'll be on my way. Maybe you can take it to your uncle?"

That would alleviate me having to see him; I had no way of knowing how awkward the conversation was going to be considering we hadn't seen each other since...making out and groping each other in the dark.

"I can let you inside." Skipper was already moving around me, skipping down the sidewalk on her way to the garage door. "Follow me!"

"Skipper Halbrook, what on earth do you think you're doing?" A new voice chimed in and before I could turn around, I knew it must be Penelope, Davis's sister.

Thank God. His niece was going to wind up giving me a stroke, first inviting me to dinner and now breaking into his house.

"Can I help you?" Penelope came all the way up to the stoop, arms crossed, shooting a warning look at her daughter, who was already happily punching buttons into the keypad of the motorized door.

It rose even as we stood there; she sized me up while Skipper disappeared inside the garage.

My hand went out. "Hi, my name is Juliet. I'm a friend of Thad and Mia's? I was away with Davis this past weekend and he forgot his tablet at the, erm. Hotel?" Hotel sounded so much better than camper; I didn't want her getting the wrong idea. "I was brining it by and your daughter saw me and came over."

Penelope visibly relaxed. "Oh yes, you're Juliet. I heard about you from my brother. Why don't you come inside, it's getting dark out—I'm not sure why the house is so dark inside, I know he's home." She followed the path that her daughter had gone; I trailed along behind her reluctantly. She glanced at me as she walked. "Were you there when he cooked his eyebrow off?"

I'd laughed. Indeed, I had been there.

Penelope and I had gone inside, where the pair of them

had semi-grilled me about Davis, and just as Skipper was asking if I was her uncle's girlfriend, he'd come strolling into the kitchen as handsome as I remember him being.

Better looking (but with one eyebrow), of course.

Who would have guessed that when I stepped inside this house tonight I would find out that my best friend had gotten engaged. Oh, how I would have loved to be there!

I wonder if it was filmed.

Juliet, she would have sent you the video already if there was one.

I am still standing next to Davis once the video chat has ended, our shoulders still touching, still breathing the same air.

He radiates heat.

"Guess you're going to be seeing more of me, hey?" he finally says with a smile.

"What do you mean?"

"Thad is my best friend, you're Mia's best friend. Best man, maid of honor..."

That makes me laugh. "I would never presume that I'd be part of the wedding party—maybe they'll elope to some tropical island. Or have the wedding in their woodland tent."

"God, that would be horrible. Don't get me wrong, last weekend was a good time, but...no it wasn't."

We both say 'no it wasn't' at the same time and find ourselves laughing again.

"I hated every minute of that trip," I say.

"Every minute?"

Well, perhaps not every minute.

"I don't think you should lie, Juliet Robertson."

When he says my name like that—low and deep and gravelly—the name sounds so...sexy.

"Alright," I admit. "Maybe not every minute of it was horrible. I did enjoy the marshmallows and chocolate."

Liar, liar, pants on fire.

Our shoulders and arms are still touching.

It would be so easy for me to turn and be in his arms; all I have to do is pivot on my heels.

My feet are killing me and I don't usually wear heels to work—and I hadn't. Just so happens I had these babies in my backseat and threw them on before heading over here on the off chance Davis was home...

Picked out this outfit specifically because I knew I was coming here.

Wanted him to think I look pretty. Wanted him to...

"Chocolate and marshmallows, my ass," he grumbles, his hand reaching around my waist and pulling me close. "Come here, you—I've wanted to kiss you since I walked into the kitchen."

"You did?"

Rather than nodding, he lowers his head.

"Are you about to kiss me?" I blurt out. I have zero chill and the words come pouring out of my mouth, stomach a nervous ball of nervousness.

Ugh.

"Yes?" He looks down at me. "Or no?"

His confusion causes bubbles of laughter to leave my throat. "I'm sorry, I'm bad at this."

Going on my tiptoes, I put my arms around his neck, this new person who feels like...

Home.

Haven't been on a date with him, but here we are, about to kiss in his kitchen, his niece and sister in the house next door.

Davis's hands go to my waist, moving them up and down my hips, stopping as he begins feeling around.

"What's this?"

There is an eyeliner pencil in the pocket of my dress—yes,

the dress has pockets, isn't that the best? Another thing I hadn't worn to school besides heels? Eyeliner.

I'd applied it in the car on the way over, then tucked it in my pocket before climbing out of the car.

Reaching down, I pull it from my pocket, holding it into the small space between us. "Just this."

"Is that mascara?"

"No." Silly. "It's eyeliner. I could draw on the rest of your eyebrow now if you wanted me to."

Davis scoffs. "You keep bringing it up, I'm beginning to think you actually want to have at it."

I mean—might as well. Maybe it would cut some of this sexual tension in the room? I'm a moron sometimes, so I open my mouth and confirm it.

"I'm willing to see if it would help, even though they're coming in quite nice." I reach up and run my finger along his face where a fully formed eyebrow used to be.

"What's that called when women have their brows tattooed on?"

"Microblading."

My back is up against the counter when he plants his hands on the small of my waist, hefting me up and setting me on the cold, granite surface so we're eye-to-eye. Pulling the eyeliner from my skirt pocket, I remove the cap.

Legs spread, he stands between them.

"Hold still."

Gently and with precise strokes, I make tiny marks on his skin that resemble hairs, one by one, as his hands splay on my waist, fingers moving in circles over the fabric of my dress.

This is some weird, effed up kind of foreplay, pardon my French.

The playful kind.

"That tickles." Davis's voice is low, his fingers dragging up and down my ribcage, teasing my body as I do my best not to ruin the progress I'm making on this brow.

"Does it?" I pause so I can look him in the eye. "Where else are you ticklish?"

"Feet. Armpits. The usual places."

The usual places. Hmm. "Guess I can explore those places later."

The comment is offhanded, meant to be a joke—but judging by the look on his face, he's stunned the words came out of my mouth. Who knew I had it in me to be that forward or flirtatious?

Not me.

Not him.

My fingers guide the pencil, my palm gently rests on his cheekbone to steady my hand—as it slides to the right, Davis's eyes slide closed as if he wants to feel the movements or at least bask in the fact that I'm touching him.

"Is it weird that I'm enjoying this?"

I giggle softly. "Is it weird that I'm oddly satisfied with the work I've accomplished here? It looks so real."

"I don't think anything is normal about the way we met or the way we became friends," he finally says once he opens his eyes again.

They're dark brown—the deepest of darks and I wonder why I've never quite noticed how intense they are; or when he had two brows how severe they looked. Severe but not stern. Davis has a friendly face even though it's incredibly masculine. Square jawline. Stubble because he hasn't shaved. He is so incredibly handsome—one of the most handsome men I've ever kissed in my life.

"Friends." I like the sound of that.

"Friends that have kissed." He leans forward and I have to stop what I'm doing. "Friends that kiss."

I can feel him hardening as he moves forward between my

legs, leaning closer until our breath mingles. No, I am the one closing my eyes, relishing the way his body heat feels and warms me from the outside in and the inside out, from my head to my toes.

I shiver but not from the cold.

"You cold?" he asks, noticing.

I'm not sure how to answer without trying to explain that he is the reason I'm shivering and not because of the temperature inside the house.

"Want me to warm you up?"

Yes.

Yes I do want him to warm me up. I give him the barest of nods to go ahead and kiss me; the acquiesce all he needs to move forward and take my face in the palm of his large hands, thumbs brushing the underside of my jawline so softly I shiver again.

He gets harder still, the erection pressing against the valley between my legs, counter height high but not so high we aren't at the perfect height to get down and dirty.

If he knelt, he could easily go down on me.

If he unzipped his pants, he could easily enter me.

If...

If...

I set down the eyeliner, letting it roll off the counter to the floor, and wrap my hands around Davis's neck, wanting to live in this moment should it never happen again. I loved kissing him while we were in the camper at the lake, and I love it when he puts his lips on the side of my neck now.

He trails them slowly, kissing along my jawline to the tip of my nose.

"Your skin is so smooth." He's murmuring into my hair before his lips meet mine, our tongues dancing and intertwining.

Sweet.

Hot.

Wet.

I give in to the kiss, my eyes sliding closed, doing the same thing he'd just done so I can feel every sensation being heightened. It's been so long since I've been kissed; I want to feel his tongue, the weight of his body pressing into me against the counter, the sounds we're making as we make out.

All I wanted was to bring him the tablet he had forgotten, I swear it—I hadn't meant to seduce him, or him seduce me, but here we are and it's incredible being in his arms like this.

Might have been better if we were still stranded in the woods. Stolen away and skinny dipped. Gotten lost in the forest and had wild sex like Mia and Thad had.

A pair of large hands work the buttons of my dress beginning at the prim collar, plucking them open one by one, working their way down. Davis skims his palms over my collarbone with one hand as the other moves my hair out of the way.

It gives me the chills.

So good.

He kisses my clavicle; shoulder.

Back to the curve of my neck where I love it the most.

"We should have done more of this in the woods," he mutters into my hair. "What a bunch of time we wasted being nuns."

"You must be a mind reader because I was literally just thinking the exact same thing."

"Bet you'd be sexy with pine cones in your hair."

"Mmhmm. Or pine needles stuck to your ass?" I'm warming to this game the same way my flesh is being warmed by his hands.

"For sure pine needles stuck to my ass. Or poison ivy."

"Sap on my tits." Is that me moaning or has my hearing gone sex-crazed, too?

My head lolls lazily as Davis's hands roam around my body, hidden inside the top of my dress.

"You know..." he begins to say. "This is fun and all but we might be more comfortable somewhere else."

My gaze shifts to the room adjacent to the kitchen. "Like the living room?"

"Or the bedroom? Not to be forward."

"None taken." I hasten. "Let's go."

I'm not expecting it when he reaches beneath me and lifts me off the counter, holding me in his arms as if I weigh nothing and heading towards the front entrance of his house. Davis bounds up the stairs towards the second level and marches us down a long hallway to a double set of doors.

He shoves one open with the toe of his foot, quite Caveman like.

Bed unmade, he dumps me in the center of it.

The mattress dips beneath our weight; the sheets rustle as we get settled.

Davis moans when his back hits the mattress, joining me.

"It feels so good to be here with you." He pulls me into him, arms going around me and to my backside. Fingers squeezing my ass as his lips find mine.

I moan, excited.

This whole thing with him is the most exciting thing to happen to me in a long string of assholes.

The hand sliding up my leg is a soft, gentle caress beneath my skirt. The thick bulge I felt in the kitchen nestles into the valley between my legs, too many clothes between us.

I find the hem of his shirt and tug it until he gets the hint, sitting up so he can slide it up and off and toss it to the floor.

It disappears in the dark.

Selfish and greedy, my hands skim him everywhere, discovering all the scars across his skin. His nipples. The hair smattered across his muscular chest.

189

He's breathing hard now and we're only touching each other in that exploratory way you do when you're naked with someone for the first time, taking them in, observing them, feeling them—feeling them on you.

Every touch is a new sensation you're sharing together.

Davis can't quite figure out how to remove my dress, so I do it. Now laying here in just my bra and underwear, I know they won't be on my body for long, either.

My fingers go to the zipper of his jeans.

"Let's get these off of you, too." I lower the zipper and slide the pants down his legs, wanting them off. Off, off, off.

Naked.

Skin on skin.

My fingers are greedy as they brush over his bare body; he is banged up and bruised and I'm grateful for that because my body is far from perfect—there are things I want to work on that I'd prefer he not see but those are my own insecurities.

They fade when I notice little things about him that I would have thought I wouldn't see; like the way his stomach isn't flat. And the fact that he doesn't have a six-pack the way I'd assumed he would. Or the long scar on his abdomen where he must have had his appendix out.

I'm glad Davis is human and not a supermodel.

I don't think I could live with that.

Reaching down toward the foot of the bed, he pulls the white, down comforter up and I hunker down underneath it, cozy and snug as a sexual little bug, grabbing him by the shoulder and pulling him beneath it, too.

We kiss again, laying on our sides, all of our tastiest bits pressed against one another.

His dick burrows between my legs.

His hands roam.

His breath quickens.

Rolling so he's braced with one arm on either side of my

head, Davis does a plank above me. I kiss his left arm at the bicep. Sniff it, wanting to inhale and memorize the smell of him. Pressing my lips against it.

He feels huge resting above me and this whole night feels... monumental.

"Goddamn, you're sexy." His mouth meets my shoulder, planting kisses there.

"I *feel* sexy."

He is sexy.

His hands are as they caress my breasts, over and under and down my side boob. Fingertip circles my nipple.

I could get off on that.

Davis's dick—that I assessed as soon as he slid his pants off —is average, thank god, and eases into me slowly when I spread my legs, no theatrics or giant cocks not fitting to ruin our moment—whoever said bigger is better hasn't met me. Give me an average dick any day and I'll be happy.

Davis's face is glorious as the range of emotions pass over it.

Ecstasy.

Bliss.

Pleasure.

His sharp intake of breath when he slides into me as deep as he can go has me gasping, too. My breath is labored as soon as he enters me, my head tipped back against the pillow as he begins rotating his hips, pressing into my pelvis with his.

Deeper.

More. "More."

He goes deeper.

Deeper still, tentatively, but surely.

"Yeah, like that," I encourage him with words, lifting my hips off the mattress, so his dick hits me where I want it most.

"That feel good?" He's moaning, voice dipping low into my ear, through my cerebellum, straight to my pussy.

Huge turn-on. Raging lady boner. "Feels so so good."

"You're so tight, Juliet." He's moaning into my hair now, fingers raking through it too, gripping my mane just tight enough so it's not painful. "Fuck, Juliet. God, you feel good."

It's pretty damn perfect.

Back and forth; push and pull.

Hips, lips, bit of teeth.

Tingles ebbing and flowing through my veins and brimming to life an orgasm that promises to be explosive.

First mine.

Then his.

We've barely worked up a sweat—it hadn't taken long at all to reach this point—lying there next to each other once he rolls off my body, head on the pillow beside mine.

He reaches for my hand.

We lay there breathing heavy, both of us staring up at the ceiling, and every so often he gives my palm a squeeze, thumb moving up and down.

"Wow." He rolls so he can kiss me on the forehead and I preen, loving every second.

CHAPTER 11

Davis

Davis: *Finally scored your number from Mia since you forgot to give it to me last night before you rushed out.*

Juliet: *LOL I did not rush out...*

Davis: *Okay fine. Maybe I just needed a reason to message you?*

Juliet: *I see how it is—now that you have my number, you're going to abuse it? LOL*

Davis: *Probably. I get bored and lonely after seven o'clock.*

Juliet: *Ha. Only after seven, not before, not after?*

Davis: *Mostly.*

Davis: *Just texting to see if you'd heard anything about the engagement party? Details, etc?*

Juliet: *YES! So soon...! (Still cannot believe they're engaged BTW...)*

Davis: *They really pulled a party together fast.*

Davis: *They literally just got engaged!*

Juliet: *I think they're trying to tie the knot soon after the Super Bowl? Planning it for this upcoming spring? So they can honeymoon while he has a few months off.*

Davis: *Before it gets crazy again? Makes total sense. Men don't talk about this stuff, so I'm not surprised I'm just hearing about this from you.*

Juliet: *If you know anything about Mia, you will learn she is a woman of action and her parents LOVE parties... Her mom is the one throwing it. Sounds like this is going to be a pre-engagement party to let everyone know they're engaged.*

Davis: *A pre-engagement party? Are you being for real right now?*

Juliet: *They're going to tell everyone at the party that they're engaged, and then they'll have an engagement party to celebrate the actual engagement. Ha!*

Davis: *My temples are throbbing...*

Juliet: *Basically I think Mia and her parents really want to celebrate. Her father is THRILLED—he has two daughters and he wants to get them all married off.*

Davis: *As long as there's food and an open bar, I'll be happy.*

Juliet: *Doesn't party food sound SO good right now? I haven't gone grocery shopping and have nothing for a decent dinner. I stood at the counter dipping saltine crackers in peanut butter—someone come take away my adult card.*

Davis: *My favorite kind of party food is bacon wrapped anything. Oh, and tiny quiches.*

Juliet: *Shrimp cocktail.*

Davis: *MEATBALLS.*

Juliet: *Those little cups with veggies and dip...*

Davis: *You know what would be awesome?*

Juliet: *What?*

Davis: *Having someone to stand in the corner with and laugh about all the footballer wives who can't move their faces or their lips.*

Juliet: *Are you talking about someone specifically to stand with you in the corner?*

Davis: *I mean... you?*

Juliet: *DAVIS! I would never stand in the corner and make fun of people!*

Davis: *You wouldn't? Damn. Does that mean you don't want to be my date?*

Juliet: *Your date? Like—date date?*

Davis: *Don't you think that would be fun? We don't have to make fun of people, we can eat and stuff. Pretend to be food reviewers...*

Juliet: *Hmmm. I do love a good food review. And wearing pretty dresses.*

Davis: *When is this fancy shindig? Do we know?*

Juliet: *This weekend, actually.*

Davis: *Are you my official invitation?*

Juliet: *Guess so. I'm spreading the word to a whole one person.*

Davis: *Surely you and Mia have other friends!*

Juliet: *Nope, just each other.*

Davis: *Seriously?*

Juliet: *No, I'm totally kidding. We're part of a group that met in high school and we are all still friends.*

Davis: *Oh, ha ha—thank god, for a second there I thought you were being serious.*

Juliet: *It wouldn't be the worst thing in the world if we were each other's only friends, there are people like that.*

Davis: *So is that a yes? Will you be my date?*

Juliet: *Yes—I think it would be fun.*

Davis: *I mean...we've already had sex so we're past that awkward 'getting to know you phase,' right?*

Juliet: *I was hoping you wouldn't bring that up...*

Davis: *I almost always bring up things that are super awkward. It's my thing. It's what I do. In fact, I can't wait for Skipper to be a teenager so I can embarrass her.*

Juliet: *Just like a dad would do.*

Davis: *Yeah, I guess I've been like a father figure to her.*

Juliet: *You guess? Or you HAVE?*

Davis: *Have. They've either lived WITH me at one point or lived NEXT to me at one point.*

Juliet: *This may be too personal, but where is her 'real' dad?*

Davis: *Honestly? Don't know. Penelope never talks about him.*

Juliet: *Do you know who the father is??*

Davis: *I have my suspicions but no, I actually don't know who it is. She was dating a few people back in college—when she got pregnant, but never brought anyone home. And those times I went to visit she never introduced me to anyone, so...*

Davis: *It's technically none of my business so I've never pushed her to find out. But now that Skipper is getting older, she's starting to ask questions. For her sixth birthday last year she told Penelope she wanted to invite her dad. It was brutal, man.*

Juliet: *I bet. No one wants to disappoint a child.*

Davis: *I feel like at this point, Penelope feels like it's impossible to contact the guy after this long. She feels like she waited too long. She's never SAID that but that's the general feeling I get.*

Davis: *It's not something I like to bring up—she's hypersensitive about it.*

Juliet: *I'm sure she feels like she has a lot to lose by talking about it.*

Davis: *Yeah—she feels like she'll lose Skipper*

Juliet: *I can see how that would instill fear into her.*

Davis: *And I know what you're thinking: if she doesn't tell the guy and he finds out somehow, she's going to lose Skipper anyway.*

Juliet: *Is that what I was thinking?*

Davis: *It's what I'M thinking. LOL*

Juliet: *But you're too scared to tell that to her face because you don't want to push her away?*

Davis: *Wow. You're good at this.*
Juliet: *Reading people is part of my job.*
Davis: *You read kids for a living.*
Juliet: *Yes, but kids turn into adults...*
Davis: *No truer words.*

CHAPTER 12

Davis

"... **W**ant to thank you all for coming. Dinner will be served shortly, please just enjoy a drink on the house."

Mia's father is loudly boasting at the front of the room, clearly enjoying the laughs he's garnering from the crowd of friends and family gathered to celebrate—or find out about—the newly engaged couple.

If anyone is wondering what the occasion is, the cake, customized Mia and Thad drinks, and CONGRATULA-TIONS banner should have given it away the second they walked in.

Still, there's going to be an announcement. And speeches. And plenty of food.

I steal an olive from a tray as it passes, skipping the drink it's planted in, nibbling on the toothpick afterwards. I already have a drink in my hand—a Manhattan that has had the shit muddled out of it—sipping it as I make my way through the crowded room.

"For such short notice, this place is packed," I say to Juliet as I approach her, taking in her hair, dress and smooth legs for the millionth time tonight.

She turns to face me, chin tilted up.

So pretty.

She looks beautiful tonight and I can't help think how strange it is seeing her all decked out and dolled up. More so than she was this past week after a day of work and definitely more than at the lake when she basically wore the same exact thing for three days straight.

"I can't get over the fact that they know this many people."

There must be over a hundred people here, only a handful that I recognize or worked with.

"Um, Mia's mother is Italian, of course there are a billion people here. She has almost eighty first cousins."

Ah, that makes sense.

I take a swallow of my drink, stirring it up, trying to get a hunk of cherry.

I'm starving, man.

We wander the crowd, nodding at people Juliet seems to be acquainted with, saying hello to people I know. She hugs a few people that bear a striking resemblance to her best friend —cousins? siblings?—as I guide her toward the appetizer spread that's inconveniently located on the opposite side of the room.

So close, *but so far away...*

I can see the stuffed mushroom and bacon wrapped asparagus from here.

Wait.

No.

Don't eat the asparagus, dude, your pee will stink later.

So what? It's not like her face is going to be in the toilet while you're taking a piss.

Okay, but what if her mouth is on your dick later?

That's putting the cart before the horse if I've ever seen it.

Eat it.

Don't eat it—there's plenty of other shit to binge on.

But you love bacon. And you love asparagus...

Why are you talking to yourself?

My arm is reaching for the table before I'm even a foot away, eyes scanning the rest of the buffet even as my hands are taking hold of a mini quiche. I grab a plate—put it down and grab a bigger one—trying to be calm and collected, so I don't look rude even as my stomach rolls. I've been preparing for this feast all day, watched what I ate so I could eat whatever splurges they were serving tonight.

Mia's family did not disappoint.

Finger foods galore including bruschetta, anti-pasta with salami and prosciutto, loads of vegetables, mozzarella on toothpicks with tomato and oil (my favorite), and a few things I don't know the names of, but that are going inside my mouth.

"You sure you don't want to save room for the actual meal?" Juliet is watching me with raised brows, eyeballing my full plate.

"Trust me, there's plenty of room for an entire meal."

Steak, lasagna—whatever they throw at me I'm going to eat.

Juliet shrugs and loads up her plate too. "This is fun, isn't it?"

It is.

She's so cute.

"Did I tell you how nice you look tonight?"

She glances up, blushing. "You did, but thank you."

It looks as if she's had her hair done for the occasion by a professional, maybe even added some extensions; it looks longer than it normally does, hanging straight down her back in a shiny long sheet. Juliet looks as romantic as her name implies, the soft layers of her petal pink dress flowing wistfully about her with every motion she makes.

Tied at the waist by a long corded belt, the flirty long sleeves billow dramatically and are fitted from the forearm to her wrist; it's covered in gold bracelets that match the large hoops in her ears.

The dress has a flattering, off the shoulder neckline.

Perfect for kissing.

"You do. I said nice but you look beautiful. I meant beautiful."

Her head lowers bashfully. "Thank you."

My hand goes to her back in an effort to be affectionate; PDA is cool at this point, right? She's not exactly throwing me off of her and this is a date?

We didn't clarify in our text messages, but when I asked her to be my date tonight, I meant romantically. What if she thought I meant 'just as friends'?

I clear my throat after swallowing something delicious. "Thanks for being my date tonight."

She laughs, nibbling on a piece of bruschetta. "No problem. We were both going to end up here anyway."

When Juliet brushes past me, skirt swaying—I inhale the smell of her perfume and follow after her like the love sick puppy I'm becoming, and it's not because of the food on her plate.

She is kind and funny and I like being around her.

I think Juliet is someone I can trust.

She can trust me, too.

Not that she has the same kind of trust issue's I have, but I know she has issues of her own. Don't we all have things we're dealing with and working through? She and I are no different.

Weaving through, she sets her plate at an unoccupied

table, pulling out the chair before I can do it for her, dammit. Plops down as I follow suit.

We're left alone to our own devices as if we were on an actual date, not a single soul coming to join us. Then again, there are about fifty roundtop tables in this ballroom—a modest restaurant, nor bar would do for Mia's parents— plenty of room for us to sit here ourselves.

"This is quite the spectacle."

Juliet's smile is sweet. "Imagine what the wedding would be like if they were going to take a full year to plan it. Oy."

"I don't even want to think about it."

"I'm pretty sure when her sister got married, there were closer to a thousand guests." She pops a bacon wrapped water chestnut in her mouth and bites off the end. "I was there and it was wild."

"You're sure they don't want to wait?"

"Honestly, who would want this chaos? I think Mia wants to avoid this fiasco. She's willing to let them have this day, then again with the bridal showers and that hoopla—but I think her goal is to spare them the expense of a huge wedding." Juliet leans forward and pours herself a glass of water from the carafe on the table. "Of course, her parents don't know this yet."

"For the record, my vote is Cancun."

"Cheers to that." She holds up her glass and we toast, clinking her water glass and my Manhattan, sipping them down happily.

My hand itches to take hers. Or at least move it from the table to her thigh beneath the table, but I'm not brave enough to make that move yet.

You had sex, idiot—she likes you.

Still.

This is different.

We were both feeling a certain kind of way the other night,

led by emotions and hormones and who knows what else. Why am I so insecure about this thing with Juliet?

I pick at my plate, setting down the stuffed mushroom I was about to inhale and wipe my fingers on the napkin in my lap.

"You know, for someone who came here on a mission to hate Thad, you sure are doing a shitty job of it." I say it with a smile, referencing all the doubt she had about her best friend's fiancé in the beginning.

Her cheeks flush again. "I never hated him—I hated what I thought he might be, which he turned out not to be."

"What did you think he was?"

"A player."

That put a grin on my face. "I mean, technically he is."

"Not a football player," she explains. "A guy who sleeps around."

"I knew what you meant."

She throws her napkin at me. "You brat."

I lean forward to kiss her on the cheek, lingering there long enough to nuzzle the tip of my nose beneath her earlobe, but not so long I'm being a clingy creep.

She blushes and smiles, thank God. "You smell good."

I do? "I showered, so... yeah." Aftershave and cologne and all that good shit I do when I'm grooming my bad self.

"What cologne do you wear?"

Uh, good question. "It's in a dark blue bottle."

That makes her laugh. "You've never looked when you were buying it?"

I can't tell her my ex-girlfriend gave it to me as a gift and I get lots of compliments on it, so I keep wearing it, but in hindsight, perhaps I should throw the whole damn bottle in the trash and go shopping for something new.

Erase the old memories.

"It was a gift and I just threw it in the drawer."

Juliet nods and nibbles on more of her appetizers, eventually pushing the plate away. "I think I should stop. It looks like everyone is taking their seats."

Many of the guests are still circulating and a slew of them are crowded near the bar—looks like a bunch of male cousins if I had to guess—but for the most part they're all taking seats, servers milling around, collecting the plates and silverware from the appetizers portion of the day.

"I know what you're thinking," Juliet says. "Yes, all this family does is eat. If you keep hanging around, you're going to gain ten pounds and so is Thad."

"Lucky bastard." I pat my full gut as a server comes around to our side of the table, asking if I'm finished with my plate. "I better be or I'll explode when I eat dinner."

We're joined by two other older couples at this ten top, seated on the other side that seemingly have zero interest in chatting or making small talk.

Fine by me, more Juliet to myself.

Before dinner, Mia's father stands and gives his blessing to the happy couple, praising Thad for *"knowing a good thing when he sees it and not being fool enough to let a woman like Mia slip through his fingers."*

Everyone raises their glass to toast as the champagne flows; literally flows in a fountain by the appetizer buffet, something I've only ever seen in movies.

While dinner is being served, Mia's brother Anthony stands and gives a speech, then her sister, Maria.

"Little sister, I am so excited you found someone to spend the rest of your life with—the same way I found my Markie." She blows her husband a kiss, a man with two toddlers on his lap who looks as if he could use a good night's sleep. *"Now Mama will stop nagging you to find a man and settle down although we both know she'll never stop nagging about something."*

Everyone finds her hilarious.

In fact, all of tonight's entertainment comes in various forms of family members standing and speaking, kissing the happy couple, drinking, speeches and eating. Thad has been kissed by more old women tonight than I've ever seen him kissed before, young and old notwithstanding.

The poor dude looks shellshocked as he lifts his glass yet another time—we all lift our glasses another time—as cousin Gina from New York tells a story about Mia as a child and how she always found "the good ones" first.

I'm assuming she means *men*.

Mia and Thad lean into each other and kiss after every spiel and I wonder if his mouth is getting chapped at the same time I wonder where the hell his folks are and why neither of them has stood to say something yet, though that doesn't seem to be his parents' style. The spotlight, I mean. From what I recall, from the few times I met his mom and dad, they're on the shyer side; never liked being interviewed by the press or filmed for television, not that I would blame them.

The media is a fickle bitch.

Then.

It's my buddy's turn to stand and make a toast; for some reason I feel as if I ought to be up there standing beside him, offering moral support or some shit.

Instead I stay put, listening beside Juliet, waiting to hear what my best friend has to say to the waiting crowd of family members.

The guests, for the first time tonight, are silent as they wait for Mia's groom to open his mouth and speak. This Adonis whom they'll forever worship because:

1. He took Mia off the market, and
2. He's a professional football player

What more could a family ask for of its new favorite son?

Thad clears his throat; not once, but twice, before fiddling with the necktie that's no doubt choking him.

"Thank you all for being here, my name is Thaddeus Dumont." The crowd laughs, and he looks down at Mia. She reaches up and squeezes his hand with a smile. Positively radiant and beaming with joy.

Thad takes a huge breath, sucking it into the microphone and causing the speakers to emit a loud, high-pitched screeching sound.

Everyone flinches.

"Sorry." His laugh is one of embarrassment and I know he's wishing he would get swallowed up whole by the floor. Still, my bud isn't a quitter and he powers on. "I haven't known Mia long, it's true. But like her father said, I knew a good thing when I saw it and I wasn't about to let her slip through my fingers. Before our first date, I asked her on our second. And on our second date, I asked her on our third. And one night when we were texting—I was traveling for work—she asked why I didn't wait like most men did. I said, 'I'm not about to let this opportunity pass me by.' I know that sounds strange and all because people aren't opportunities, but I didn't mean it like that. I meant; the opportunity of something good. The opportunity of something real and permanent. I knew the second I laid eyes on Mia that she was an opportunity for the life my parents have and that's what I want and I wasn't about to waste it by playing games. And I wasn't about to waste another minute not asking her out."

Around the room, eyes begin to dampen.

A few lips begin to quiver, including mine.

"Shit," I mutter, lifting the napkin on my lap to swipe at my moist eyes.

"I don't know what I'm saying—I didn't come with a speech prepared. All I know is what's in my heart and my heart was telling me not to wait a second longer to ask Mia to be my wife."

I can't hold it in any longer.

The floodgates open and I cry as hard as any woman in the room, blubbering into my napkin like a damn fool, among one of few men crying actual tears.

I'm sensitive, okay, I can't help myself!

That doesn't make me weak, it makes me...makes me...

Oh fuck, I never should have raised my eyes to look at Granny and I shouldn't have raised my eyes to look at Juliet because hers are wide and shocked as they stare back at me.

"Oh wow, Davis, are you okay?"

"I'm fine. Don't look at me, I'm hideous," I grumble, wanting to ugly cry in peace.

God, why am I like this?

WHO MADE ME THIS WAY?

Juliet's hand goes to my back as she gently massages my shoulders; it's a move I lean into, basking in the physical contact. It's been days since she and I kissed, days since we had sex, too many days.

"You're such a sweet man," she's saying as she rubs my back, whispering that it's going to be okay, which only makes me sniffle harder. "Are you sad your best friend isn't going to be around as much?"

Huh? No.

"That's not why I'm crying," I pout with a stuffed nose.

"Then what's wrong?"

"I just..." Ugh, how do I put this? "Love weddings."

In fact, you can put money on the fact that I'm going to be a loud, crying, whimpering mess at Thad's nuptials, *guaranteed.*

"You love weddings? Or you love love?"

Both, I guess. "Yes. I'm one sappy bastard."

"That's so cute."

Cute? Sweet?

Blah!

Over Juliet's head, my eyes lock with Thad as he raises his glass again—towards me—that knowing look on his face says it all.

The same thing that happened to him is happening to me.

CHAPTER 13

Juliet

"Thanks for bringing me home tonight, Davis, I had a really great time."—*Things you say on a date even if you don't know whether it's romantic or not.*

He said all the right things: called me beautiful, told me I look nice.

Did all the right things: kissed my cheek, nuzzled my ear.

Smelled good. *Sounded* wonderful. Laughed and cried at all the right times and was a wonderful partner throughout the entire night.

We had a great time; even danced, something I haven't done since, well—PROM.

We're shuffling up the front walkway of my little rental, the lights on the porch come on automatically at six o'clock sharp, day in and day out. They're glowing now in the cold, desperate for the holiday decorations I'll be able to put out in a few months' time without appearing crazy to the neighbors.

Twinkling lights.

Snowflakes.

Candy canes, who knows where the season will take me!

It's not so cold I'm wearing my jacket; Davis insisted on

walking me to the front door. Insisted on carrying my coat, too, like a true gentleman, and I can't remember the last time a man has held a door, let alone my jacket.

I want to twirl and twirl, my mind reeling, wanting to kick myself for the negative thoughts I'd had about Thad and Davis when they both turned out to be decent dudes.

Better than decent. I mean, who knew Davis would be a crier?

Confession: *I had a wee bit of secondhand embarrassment watching him sniffle through the last of the speeches, if I'm being honest...*

As per usual, I'm barreling down the sidewalk before I realize there is no one beside me, the space where Davis once occupied is empty. Confused, I look around.

Find him down on one knee in the middle of the walkway.

"Juliet Robertson, I have something to ask you."

It one hundred percent looks like he's about to propose. Racing forward, I try to pull him to a stand, but he isn't budging.

"Oh my god, what the hell are you doing? Get up."

Davis rolls his eyes. "I'm not proposing, calm down."

My body relaxes.

"Thank god." I hasten to add, "No offense."

"None taken? I don't think. I mean, I'm slightly offended but I'll get over it."

But for real—what is he doing kneeling on the damn ground!

My heart and head are racing in tandem, neither one knowing what to do or how to make sense of this strange man in front of me.

Davis Halbrook—the man with two last names for a name —is a puzzle to me.

"I have to start over because I rehearsed everything I wanted to say on the car ride over and I think it has to be in order for me to get it right—I wasn't expecting you to freak out like, immediately." Throat clears. "Juliet Robertson, I have something to ask you."

I nod regally (since he's already stated this is *not* a marriage proposal). "Proceed."

"We've done a few things out of order. Normally I wouldn't sleep with a woman before buying her a dinner, having a nice drink, and getting to know her first. But in a way, we'd already kind of done those things at the campground."

I stand perfectly still in the middle of the concrete walk.

This sure *sounds* like it's leading up to something serious...

"That morning when I laid eyes on your sleeping, drooling face, I won't lie—I thought you were adorable."

Ew.

"...And when you loathed me upon sight, I thought it was, well—adorable."

Ugh.

"The fish hook I could have lived without." He brings a hand to his ear and tugs.

Hmm, still must be bothering him.

"The good news is, I grew on you..."

I mean—it wasn't hard. Davis is a perfectly amenable, amazing human being. Who wouldn't fall at least a little in like with him after a short while?

A fool, that's who—and Juliet Robertson is no fool.

"...the same way you grew on me."

Wait. *What?* He just said I was adorable!

Twice!

"Ha, I just wanted to see if you were listening."

"Oh I'm listening alright. I'm a captive audience." He has me hooked, needing to know what's going to come out of his mouth next, thirsty for more.

"What I'm trying to say is, we got a little off track by doing the horizontal mambo before going on a romantic first date—

banging one out does not count—but that doesn't mean we can't start over again. That's what I want—to start over."

Horizontal mambo.

Banging one out.

Start over.

"I think you're spectacular even when you're throwing up in the bushes. You're funny and outgoing and sweet."

Sweet? Outgoing? I'm not certain about that—sometimes I can be sweet, but I can also be a real, huge pain in the ass. Difficult, especially when I'm getting my period. Moody when I'm stressed out or when things aren't going great at work.

However, now is not the time to squabble over details.

It's cold and he's being kind, wooing me on bended knee.

This is a first for me.

"I *propose*," he winks. "That we officially begin dating. Like with the end goal of seeing how this could work...um, long term."

I have no idea what to say. All I know is that I need him to rise and get up off the ground, so I can go up on my tiptoes and kiss him—kiss him as hard as we kissed in his kitchen the other night while I was painting on his eyebrow.

"Would you please stand up?" I'm growing impatient as he kneels there, the giant goof and his grand gesture.

"Okay, but you haven't answered my question."

"Did you ask a question?"

Davis shifts on his knee, looking slightly uncomfortable. "Juliet Robertson, would you do me the honor of dating me?"

I tap my chin in thought. "And where are we going on this first date of ours?"

"I don't know—I was thinking we could do something fun, like crash a wedding?"

"Davis Halbrook, we are not crashing a wedding!"

"What if it's our friends' wedding?"

"Sure, that would be great, but that wedding isn't for a

few weeks and were you planning on waiting a few weeks to take me on a proper date?" I tap my heel on the concrete. It clicks in the evening air.

"Valid point."

"How about we go to a movie?"

He considers this, still on the ground. "That would be fine if we could talk the entire time, which we can't."

Okay, so—no to the movies. Sheesh. "Dinner and bowling?"

That cheers him up. "You like to bowl?"

"No, but that's the first thing that popped into my head when I opened my mouth."

He finally stands, sliding him arms around my waist, making me feel cute and adorable and sexy. "I can watch you tiptoe down the lane and toss that big bowling ball."

I eyeball him suspiciously. "Will you let me spray the finger holes with hand sanitizer?"

"Um, sure?"

That makes me happy. If I have to go bowling and look like a fool, at least I won't have to stick my fingers into petri dishes.

"Great, then it's settled, we have a date and we're going bowling."

We stand outside grinning like fools until a gust of wind billows my skirt and sends a freezing cold puff that causes me to shiver.

"Brrr." I glance up at Davis through my lashes. "Do you want to come inside for a little bit?" Or longer? Overnight will work just fine, I don't have to be up in the morning. "It's getting so cold, I'm not sure how much longer I can stand out here and pretend not to freeze my ass off."

"Sure, I could come in for a bit."

Leading him inside through my modest doorway, into my modest entryway, and my modest little two bedroom home, I feel a twinge of self-consciousness. Yes, it's my very own place but:

1. I don't own it, and
2. His place is so much grander than mine

I doubt he cares. I know he's not judging me, but his place is so huge compared to mine. My house is like a dollhouse compared to his.

I flip on lights as I move down the little hallway toward the kitchen then flip that light on, too. Davis trails behind me quietly, and I can hear him removing his sport coat and hanging it on the hook near the door. After that, I hear him removing his shoes and placing them on the mat.

Bending, I unbuckle the straps of my high heels—it feels heavenly taking those off. I don't wear them often and my feet are killing me, especially since we danced tonight.

It's more cardio than I've done in ages, ha ha.

"This is a cute place," he tells me as he makes his way into my small living room.

Every so often I jokingly refer to the living room as "The Molecule," for it only has space for a sofa, the coffee table, and the television that's mounted on the opposite wall. There's a very small fireplace in the room—my home is turn of the century—and the bedroom has a fireplace as well. It's how they used to heat this house, but not anymore.

The landlord closed off the flue, rendering it impossible to light a fire (unless you want to burn the place down), I'm sure due to liability with renters.

Fortunately it's not a duplex and it's not an apartment.

It's a cute, nuggety, little house.

"Is this where you grade papers?" He's staring down at a pile of essays I am indeed grading, and picks one off the top of the heap. "What were they supposed to be writing about?"

"Students' choice. Anything as long as it's five hundred words, double spaced."

He skims it several more seconds before returning it to the pile.

"Seems simple enough."

Yeah—*you'd think*. Unfortunately with middle schoolers, nothing is ever as simple as you try to make it. Inevitably there will be essays in that pile that do not meet either of the criteria; some may only be written with one hundred words and will be triple spaced. Some of them will be two hundred words and single spaced. Some of them will write in such a large font, hoping to trick me into thinking they've met the criteria when in fact? They only managed to make more work for themselves than was necessary.

"Make yourself comfortable." I finish removing my shoes and place them near his by the door until I can stick them back in my closet. "Would you like anything to drink?"

Having him in my house is making me want a shot or something stiff. I'm not necessarily nervous but it is different having this large man in my space.

"Sure, do you have any bottles of water?"

"One bottle of water coming right up!" I grab two then head back into the living room to join him on the couch.

"This place is really cute," he says again, glancing around. "How long have you lived here?"

"Not terribly long. Just a little over a year, I think? Since going from elementary school to middle school—I had a small bump in pay so I thought, shit, Juliet. Treat yourself. So I moved out of my apartment and moved in here."

We both twist off the tops of our water.

"I love old historical buildings. I've always wanted to live in something mid-century. Remodel it so it retained all its retro vibes or rent it out as a vacation rental."

Dang. "Sounds like you've actually thought about this."

"I have. I have a buddy who renovates houses that also plays pro, but that's his full-time off-season gig—I'm only thinking about doing it for fun. So we'll see, there never seems to be a good time for that."

"Newsflash: there is never a good time to pull the trigger on anything. There's never a good time to schedule a trip or go out of town. There's never a good time to leave your job. There's never a good time to sell your house." I shrug, feeling wisdomy. "I say do it."

Davis laughs. "You're not wrong about that. I think the one thing I'm missing is a partner. Think it would be a hell of a lot more fun, don't you?"

Awww—he's so sentimental!

I scooch over on the couch and smooch him on the lips. The peck on his mouth turns into a sensual make out session; the kind where I inevitably end up on Davis's lap instead of on my own side of the sofa. His hand runs up the length of my calf and over my knee, until it's firmly planted beneath my skirt. His palm finds its home on my thigh, warming me to the core.

Delicious.

Tonight he smells like cologne and a little bit of sweat from dancing and being in a room crowded full of people— which isn't a bad thing. I lean closer and give him another whiff: fresh air from standing outside and talking before I invited him in.

"I never showed you a grand tour of the place," I moan as his fingers trace my pussy over the satin fabric of my panties.

He teases the apex between my thighs. "I'm taking a tour of your place right now."

"I meant the *bed*room."

He nods, standing and lifting me up all in one motion, giant of a man he is, and my breath catches from the excitement of being with him.

It's always exciting being with him...

The whole thing feels like deja vu as he carries me into the bedroom, pushing through the door with the tip of his toe, and deposits me in the center of my bed. *Thank god it's a queen* because there's no way this man would fit on a full size mattress.

He's way too big and he's way too tall. His feet would stick out the other end.

We get busy shucking our clothes; there's no need to be coy about it, we both know we're going to end up naked in the end so why prolong the inevitable?

"You are so damn sexy," he whispers. "Have I told you tonight how beautiful you look?"

"Only a few times," I laugh. "But do go on."

"You're so beautiful, Juliet—how did I get so lucky?"

I am melting in this man's arms. "How did you get so lucky?" Is he out of his mind? I'm the one who is lucky!

I was a complete shrew the first day that we met, wanting to see things about Davis that were not there and I was bitter and jealous of my best friend.

Oh, I played it off well. Never would have admitted it to myself a month ago when Mia was asking me on the getaway trip but we all know that's exactly what was happening. The reason I was trying not to like her boyfriend—now fiancé—was because I didn't want to lose her, not because he was a bad person. I was scared I would be left behind.

I'm self-aware enough to know all of this about myself.

I am so lucky Davis laughed off all my pouting. The puking. The fish hook in the side of his head.

I kiss his ear now, the injury where I had accidentally run a piercing piece of metal through his lobe barely noticeable. It has healed beautifully.

Davis basks in the attention I'm giving him right now, his hands roaming slowly over my skin as we lay on top of my covers. Thankfully I keep the thermostat set at seventy degrees, so I'm not cold; his body is a blazing inferno and keeping us both toasty.

He trails kisses down my neck. Over my collarbone, down my sternum between the center of my breasts. His lips trail kisses over my belly to my belly button, hands lowering too, reaching so they're beneath my ass.

I shift on the mattress, propping myself on the pillow, so I can watch his journey south, reveling at the sight of his dark hair, soon to be between my legs.

His warm mouth drags along the sensitive flesh of my thighs. Warm tongue. Wet tongue.

Thumbs graze over my pussy, making small circles over my clit, round and round and round they go until I moan, tipping my head back, soft moan leaving my throat.

Oh that feels good...

It's been s-so long...

Yes, Davis, right there...

He's so good at this, so good at this, so good...

Harder though, just a little, not so gentle. I want to feel it. I want to burn.

I thrash my head, wanting him to climb up my body and slide his dick inside me—at the same time I want him to keep going. It's never been easy for me to come when a man is going down on me; I used to not have them even bother to try. But this is different and I know I'm going to, I can f-f-feel it.

Oh shit...

Yes, just like that...

Less tongue, more sucking, oh shit yessssss...

My body is blazing hot; on fire.

I want to open my mouth and say something—I open my mouth and encourage him, but he's already doing an outstanding job on his own without my guidance. Plunging my fingers through his hair, I tug gently—gently *so he knows* I am euphoric. So he knows I am enjoying this.

So he knows how turned on I am.

Davis's arms splay, elbows spreading me wider, one of his palms spread on my pelvis, pushing down gently as his mouth sucks and licks.

Oh god.

Oh Davis...

OH...O...

After I come, he moves up my body, sliding into me with a loud groan, thrusting and thrusting and thrusting.

Moaning.

Kissing my neck.

I raise my hips, still sensitive, still reeling from my orgasm, hoping I can ride the wave of another one, searching for that spot as he pumps into me—knowing it's there.

Just a little more...

Keep going, don't stop.

"Oh fuck, Juliet..."

Keep going, don't stop.

More, more, more.

"I'm close," he groans.

"Don't stop," I tell him.

I'm close, too, and I know if he keeps going I will come again, and I want this second orgasm so fucking bad I can literally taste it in my mouth.

Don't stop, don't stop, I silently plead, not wanting to be a complete sex monster, especially considering he just went down on me and I've already come once.

I am one lucky brat.

Juliet 2, Davis 1

CHAPTER 14

Davis

I'm not surprised to see my sister in my living room when Juliet and I walk through the door to my house after our first official date. After all, our two houses are side by side, and my sister loves my place better than hers because of the state-of-the-art kitchen and larger size; more room to roam, she always says.

Plus, as a single mom, I think she feels safer in my space. So they hang out here as often as they like and feel right at home, crashing without an invitation.

Like tonight.

I was hoping to come inside then come inside Juliet, not come inside and have to see my sister.

She looks over her shoulder at us from the couch in the nearby living room when we enter the kitchen, barely sparing us a cursory glance. Whatever television show has her transfixed is getting her full attention.

"I just put Skipp to bed—she tried to stay awake until you got home but her little eyeballs couldn't fight it anymore."

"Really? It's so early." Only seven o'clock.

I remove my coat and toss it on the barstool in the kitchen. "She up in the guest bedroom?"

"She was at a friend's house today with an indoor pool. They swam and swam until their arms were noodles and their skin was all wrinkly. She's beat."

"Bet she'll be up at the ass crack of dawn though."

"She'll for sure be up at the ass crack of dawn." My sister laughs knowingly. "I made chicken for dinner if you're hungry."

Penelope is sitting in jeans, cross-legged on the couch, long, dark hair in a messy bun, snuggly pink sweatshirt on her body.

"We ate a few hours ago, but it smells delicious," Juliet says, taking an empty spot next to Penelope on the couch. She dressed up for our date, black leather pants, killer high heels, and a floral blouse; we thought it was hilarious when she had to put on bowling shoes.

"Then we had pizza while we were bowling." I laugh. "And appetizers. For some reason I caught a second wind once I started kicking her ass and taking names."

Juliet rolls her eyes in my direction. "Okay, let's brag about it, we had the gutter guards up."

"Doesn't matter," I argue.

"Actually...it does."

"Are we always going to squabble like this?" I muse hopefully, walking over to join them, plopping down beside Juliet and picking up her legs, setting them across my lap. I immediately begin massaging her feet.

"Is that what this is? A squabble?"

My sister is watching us now with an amused expression. "Aww, aren't the two of you just adorable."

"I'd lean over and ruffle your hair, but you're too far."

"Good, I don't want my hair ruffled—I grew out of that in second grade."

"Liar. You used to love it when I would give you noogies."

"*Said no one ever.*"

Juliet laughs, resting her head back on the sofa when I apply pressure to the balls of her feet, kneading one heel then the other.

"God, that feels like heaven!" She groans. "Those shoes were killing my feet. And after the week I've had…" She groans again, closing her eyes.

It had been a week; a long one. Not because we were so excited about our date and counting down the days, but because I wound up traveling two days for work, and Juliet had a shitstorm at school and had conferences with a few students' parents that had been acting up in her classroom.

When I'd picked her up tonight, held the car door open for her, then leaned over to kiss her before putting the car in drive, she'd said, *"One of the worst parts of my job is facing a parent who had no idea their child was disrupting class. It's awful."*

She needed the night out as an escape—or reward—and I was more than happy to provide it.

Steak. Red wine.

Candlelight and chocolate cake.

The servers at the restaurant left us to talk and we'd held hands across the table; it was damn near perfect.

Bowling was, too.

Who knew I was so good at it, bumpers or not, despite Juliet's objections on the matter?!

The doorbell sounds and we all look at each other.

"Who could that be?"

"Oh shit!" Penelope pops up from the couch. "I forgot I ordered ingredients to make pancakes in the morning, we're all out of flour and vanilla."

She scurries toward the door and I run my hands up and down Juliet's legs, wiggling my eyebrows at her suggestively.

"Know what I'm thinking right now?"

"Gee, I can only imagine it has something to do with balls and holes."

Ha ha. "Good one, but also: yes. My balls, your hole."

Juliet cocks her head to the side, laughing as she says, "Honestly, Davis, I would never have pegged you for such a pervert."

I reel back, shook. "Me? When am I a pervert!"

But she's laughing. And laughing still when I lean forward and kiss her, expecting my sister to walk back through the kitchen door at any moment, bags in hand from her grocery store delivery.

Except.

When she does, she's not alone.

I hesitate only a brief second before removing Juliet's legs from my lap and standing.

That is most certainly not the DoorHub delivery guy.

I recognize the man who follows her inside the house, although we've never met. He's an athlete too; a seasoned one with a lot of years under his belt in the pros.

I rise, extending my hand.

"Sorry to show up like this unexpectedly, but I'm in town for a game and heard you still lived in the area." He removes his ball cap and runs a hand through his hair, staring down at Penelope.

Staring down at my sister, but not making eye contact with me, I might as well not even be in the room.

"My agent Rocko was able to get in touch with Silus Goodwyn," he's telling Penelope as if I were not standing there listening. "Your brother doesn't have social media, so I figured I'd pop in and see if he was willing to share your phone number—I wasn't expecting you to answer his door!"

Silus is the stadium manager where I used to play ball and also happens to be a good friend of mine—not good enough apparently, that he doesn't have the damn common sense NOT to give my goddamn address to virtual strangers!

I could give a fuck that I've seen this dude on television.

I do not know him.

I'm confused. "Do you know each other?"

I glance back and forth between the two of them, not failing to notice the color has yet to return to my sister's face.

"Are you here to see me?" I say it slowly. "Or are you here to see my sister?"

"Shit, I'm sorry." The guy extends his hand and introduces himself. "Penelope and I dated back in college—I'm not sure if she told you? Anyway, we lost touch way back and I always wonder what she's been up to." He shifts on the balls of his feet, plopping the ball cap back on his moppy hair. "I know this is weird, but I was hoping we could reconnect while I'm in town."

She's pasted on the fakest smile I've ever seen. "This sure is a surprise. How long has it been?"

"Gosh, I wouldn't even know but—" he stops talking, but looks like he has the weight of the world on his shoulders. "Look, I'm going to leave you with my card and if you want to have coffee or something. Or drinks. Or...I don't know— maybe we could have dinner at The Tower Club while I'm here and catch up?"

The Tower Club was voted the most romantic restaurant in the city three years in a row, located eighty floors in the sky in downtown Chicago.

This dude is not here to idly chitchat.

He wants something from my sister.

"Gotcha." I take the card from his fingers and stuff it in the back pocket of my slacks, ushering him back toward the front entry from whence he came, back toward the front door and the shiny black sports car parked in my front driveway.

"Good meeting you, bro. If she wants to talk, she'll be in touch."

He's staring right through me at Penelope when I close the door in his face, leaving him standing in my front yard.

What the actual fuck was that nonsense about?

I spin slowly on the balls of my feet. "Care to tell me what that was all about?"

My stomach growls—out of frustration or hunger, I do not know, but I'm going to feed it because my nerves are shot and my head needs clarity and only snacks can do that for me. Heading toward the kitchen, only Juliet trails along after me, worrying at her bottom lip with her top front teeth.

"Are you sure you don't want to check on your sister? She looks...like she's seen a ghost."

I yank open the fridge and pull out the newest member of leftovers in the Tupperware family: chicken and rice. Popping open the lid and wait for my sister to lumber into the kitchen and join us at the counter.

"What was he doing here at seven at night, Penelope?" Aimlessly, I spoon a heap of rice onto a plate, not giving a shit about rations so much as I am about occupying my hands.

"No idea. I guess he wants to...um, reconnect."

"I know who that was—how do you know who that was?" I point the wooden spoon in her direction.

That was a Pro baller.

That was a Super Bowl champion.

That was the fastest running back in the NFL league in his rookie days, blah blah blah, weren't we all fabulous at one point?

"That was..." My sister can hardly find the words, putting her face in her hands. "That was Skip Jennings."

They call him The Skip because when he would make a touchdown, he would hop through the end zone as if he were being skipped across water—

Skipper.

"I know who Skip Jennings is, Penelope. *What was he doing in my house?*"

The End

———

Find out who Skip Jennings is to Penelope Halbrook in
***The Mrs. Degree* coming in May!**
Pre-Order at your favorite retailer today!

About Sara Ney

Sara Ney is the USA Today Bestselling Author of the How to Date a Douchebag series and is best known for her sexy, laugh-out-loud New Adult romances.

Among her favorite vices, she includes: iced lattes, historical architecture, and well-placed sarcasm. She lives colorfully, collects vintage books, art, loves flea markets, and fancies herself British.

Sign up for Sara's Newsletter to find out about her book releases, and read real-life "Sara Dates A Douchebag" stories only found in her newsletter!

For more information about Sara Ney and her books, visit:
https://authorsaraney.com

Read the First Chapter from Bachelor Society

Brooks

"Eeny, meeny, miney, mo..."

I knock one of the tiny model cardboard houses off the development community layout I've been working on. Flick it with my forefinger until it flies off the board and onto the floor, landing in a corner with the rest of them.

"Catch a tiger." Flick goes another one. "By." Flick. "The." Flick. "Toe."

Flick, flick.

Five more fly off the flat board. It's large, square, an exact replica of a subdivision the architectural firm I work for is developing. Or...proposing. Or...was going to?

I'm not on the project anymore, thank God. I've been promoted—fucking *promoted*!—and moved to the project I've been salivating over since I started here. Literal drool comes out the side of my mouth when I talk about it.

I've only been at this company for one year; I rose up the ladder quicker than I'd planned, not because of nepotism or favoritism or sleeping my way to the top, but because I'm a great fucking architect.

I'm not just good at my job.

I'm great at it.

I love it.

Dream about it.

Architecture isn't only what I do for a living. It's my *passion*.

I'm not sad to see this development project leave my hands and my office. Now, if the intern, Taylor, would get his ass in here to remove this goddamn model, that would be swell. It's cluttering up all the space—I may have been promoted, but my office is still small as fuck.

Leaning forward, I hit the button on my phone's intercom and buzz the front desk. "Hey Taylor, can you come to my office to grab this community model?"

He clicks his tongue. "Will do."

"Thanks."

I swivel in my desk chair, plucking a sheet of loose paper from the printer. Fold a piece in half once, twice. Fold down each corner into a triangle, smoothing it down with my nail.

The paper airplane I've folded is a crisp, dynamic flying machine. I press it between my thumb and forefinger. Squeeze my left eye shut like I'm a four-year-old, aiming for a spot on the window in my corner office. The spot where I have the small, orange and white basketball hoop suction-cupped. My mom gave it to me as a gift, hoping it would distract me from work during the day, saying I'm too keyed up, but I don't know what good she thought a toy fucking basketball hoop was going to do for my stress level.

Whatever.

She shouldn't be spending money she doesn't have on junk.

Still. I plastered it on my office window anyway—as she

intended—when I should have thrown the dumb thing in the garbage.

Waste not, want not...

I squint again, aiming the airplane toward the target, pull it back before launching, and let it fly in a smooth arc.

Instead of hitting the backboard of the hoop, it ricochets off the glass, bounces, and falls to the ground amongst the tiny white houses.

I leave it, a heap in the graveyard of my shitty ideas.

Fuck.

I need inspiration for this new project I've been assigned to before my promotion turns into a demotion. Need to prove to my bosses that they didn't make a mistake when they trusted me with this assignment. It's a lot of pressure.

I need a fucking drink.

I need to take a piss.

Standing, I grab my cell before exiting my office to hit the restroom at the end of the hall, pushing through the door and unsnapping my jeans. There's one urinal and one toilet, and the latter is occupied—dammit. The toilet has a stall and is the perfect place to text, unlike my office, which is a veritable fishbowl of repression with its massive glass walls.

After I pee, re-zip my pants, and wash my hands, I pull out my cell, slanting against the cool tile wall for support. Tap out a message to my idiot best friends as I walk back to my office: *What time can you meet at The Basement?*

Phillip: *Yeah*

Yeah? What kind of answer is that? I'm looking for a time the bastard can meet for drinks tonight, not whether he can commit or not.

Me: *What time, dude?

Blaine isn't responding, but if Phillip and I are going for drinks, he's going to have the fear of missing out. No way will he not show.

Phillip: *Six.*

Fine, six o'clock it is. I'll be fucking starving by then, but The Basement is the closest pub to my apartment, located in the middle of my neighborhood. It's convenient, old, filled with tons of character, and in the basement of an ancient building that used to be a national bank, which is pretty fucking cool.

The Basement has appetizers and I can eat more when I get home if I'm still desperate, but actual food would be great. Either I eat or I get drunk on two.

I might have been a member of a fraternity in college, but I'm still a lightweight. Cannot handle my liquor. Have always been that way, always will be.

I return to my office, and just as I'm about to construct another paper airplane, a jaunty little knock sounds at the door; Taylor is rapping his knuckles on the glass wall, eyes trailing to the pile of houses and planes littering my carpet.

"Stressed?" He pushes a pair of black frames up the bridge of his nose.

"Very." Why lie to the kid? If he wants to be an architect once he graduates, he oughta know it's not always ribbon cutting ceremonies, fundraisers, networking, and champagne lunches.

It takes actual work.

It takes engineering, long hours, lack of a social life, and countless sleepless nights to meet deadlines.

Taylor? He still has years of hopes and happy hours and bullshit dreams ahead of him.

"I don't mean to sound bitter, I'm just having a day."

The smile he gives me is sympathetic. "We all have them."

I look over at him. "When do you have shitty days?" The guy radiates unicorns and rainbows and happiness.

He considers my question. "I have shitty days when, like, Starbucks gets my order wrong."

"Get the fuck out of here. That's not an actual problem." I laugh, bending to help him retrieve all the pieces of paper discarded on the ground.

"Where should I take this model?"

I blow a strand of dark, hair out of my eyes, mentally noting the need for a haircut, or a trim at the very least. "Conference room B, maybe? I don't think anyone is using it. Then Daniels can decide what he wants to do with this." I hand Taylor a stack of teeny houses with three-car garages. "This development is his brainchild, but I don't think he has space in his office for one more model mockup."

"Got it, boss."

I snort. "I'm not your boss." *Not even close.*

"But you could be, someday," Taylor points out, bending down to grab a paper airplane and extending as if he's going to send it sailing across the room.

I pause. He's right; I could become his boss someday if I keep working my ass off. They make associates partners around here. Technically, if I stay and work hard, there's a chance I could become one, too.

"How old are you?" Taylor asks hesitantly, scooping up a paper house.

I glance at the model of the community resting on a drafting table in the corner of my office. There must have been two hundred little houses on that giant platform, half of which are now scattered on my floor.

"Twenty-six."

"See? And you're already on a major project. It only took you a year."

Shit, is he keeping track of my career? That's...weird.

I eye Taylor suspiciously. "Are you stalking me?"

He laughs, blushing. "No!" Adjusts the bowtie around his neck. "But I'm following your career because I'm trying to learn how to become successful."

Holy shit. Wow.

I clear my throat, choking up a bit. "I'm just a guy from a crappy neighborhood, Taylor. I paid my way through college, busted my ass, took a lot of drugs to stay awake late so I could study—sometimes it's worth it, sometimes it's not."

I doubt I should be giving this kid advice. He probably came from the suburbs—not unlike the communities this architecture firm designs and develops, with two married parents, a picket fence, and a dog.

"I know what you're thinking," he finally says. "But you're wrong."

My brows go up. "Oh yeah? What am I thinking?"

"That I had it easy and was popular, got good grades *and* all the ladies."

Um—that's not what I was thinking. Close enough, though.

"Fine—my parents paid for everything and my dad got me this job, but that doesn't mean I don't want to be an architect, or that I can't be a good one. I just want someone to mentor me, someone I can relate to."

"Aren't you gay?"

"I mean at work. I don't want to follow you around *after*ward. I have a feeling your personal life is a shitshow—no offense."

"None taken." Because it is.

He nods, the thick, navy, tweed vest he has buttoned over a white dress shirt far too dressy for a Thursday, but who am I to judge? I'm wearing denim jeans for fuck's sake.

Wrinkly ones.

"So will you? Mentor me?"

"I don't know what the hell that even means."

"I'll write you a proposal."

Jesus Christ. "Proposal as in job description?"

"Exactly."

"Fine."

His excitement is evident, especially when he stands. I swear to God, the dweeb has pep in his step even as he dumps all the little houses onto the board and scoops it up from the bottom, teetering.

"Don't get your hopes up—you probably won't learn anything from me."

"That's alright. We all start somewhere."

Such optimism.

I wish I felt it too.

To read the rest of Bachelor Society, purchase at your favorite retailer now!

Also by Sara Ney

Accidentally in Love Series

The Player Hater

The Mrs. Degree coming May 2022

Jock Hard Series

Switch Hitter

Jock Row

Jock Rule

Switch Bidder

Jock Road

Jock Royal

Jock Reign

Jock Romeo

Trophy Boyfriends Series

Hard Pass

Hard Fall

Hard Love

Hard Luck

The Bachelors Club Series

Bachelor Society

Bachelor Boss

How to Date a Douchebag Series

The Studying Hours

The Failing Hours

The Learning Hours

The Coaching Hours

The Lying Hours

The Teaching Hours

#ThreeLittleLies Series

Things Liars Say

Things Liars Hide

Things Liars Fake

The Kiss & Make Up Series

Kissing in Cars

He Kissed Me First

A Kiss Like This

The Bachelor Society Duet: The Bachelors Club

Jock Hard Box Set: Books 1-3

Made in the USA
Monee, IL
22 February 2022

91598972R00142